VAMPIRE HUNTER D

Other Vampire Hunter D books published by
Dark Horse Books and Digital Manga Publishing

VOL. 1: VAMPIRE HUNTER D

VOL. 2: RAISER OF GALES

VOL. 3: DEMON DEATHCHASE

VOL. 4: TALE OF THE DEAD TOWN

VOL. 5: THE STUFF OF DREAMS

VOL. 6: PILGRIMAGE OF THE SACRED AND THE PROFANE

VAMPIRE HUNTER D

VOLUME 7
MYSTERIOUS JOURNEY TO THE NORTH SEA
PART ONE

Written by
HIDEYUKI KIKUCHI

Illustrations by
YOSHITAKA AMANO

English translation by
KEVIN LEAHY

Dark Horse Books®
Milwaukie

Los Angeles

VAMPIRE HUNTER D 7:
MYSTERIOUS JOURNEY TO THE NORTH SEA PART ONE

Cover art by Yoshitaka Amano

English translation by Kevin Leahy

Book design by Heidi Fainza

Published by
Dark Horse Books
a division of Dark Horse Comics
10956 SE Main Street
Milwaukie, OR 97222
darkhorse.com

Digital Manga Publishing
1487 West 178th Street, Suite 300
Gardena, CA 90248
dmpbooks.com

Library of Congress Cataloging-in-Publication Data

Kikuchi, Hideyuki, 1949-
 [Hokkai mako. English]
 Mysterious journey to the North sea / written by Hideyuki Kikuchi ; illustrated by Yoshitaka Amano ; English translation by Kevin Leahy.
     p. cm. -- (Vampire Hunter D; v. 7)
 "Originally published in Japan in 1988 by Asahi Sonoroma Co."--Vol. 1, t.p. verso.
 ISBN-13: 978-1-59582-107-2 (v. 1)
 ISBN-10: 1-59582-107-4 (v. 1)
 I. Amano, Yoshitaka. II. Leahy, Kevin. III. Title.
PL832.I37H6513 2007
895.6'36--dc22

                         2006102529

ISBN-10: 1-59582-107-4
ISBN-13: 978-1-59582-107-2

First printing: April 2007

10 9 8 7 6 5 4 3 2 1

Printed in the United States of America

VAMPIRE HUNTER D

A Vision of Beauty

I

After midnight, the wind grew stronger. The clouds rumbled as they rolled along. In accordance with the moon's dips undercover, the night alternated between glowing with white light and sinking into pitch blackness. Somewhere out there, something howled. It was a cry unlike any she'd ever heard, and it made the girl by the window grow stiff.

"Nothing to be scared about," said the master of the lodging house, wiping his mouth after another in a long line of cheap drinks. The unlabeled bottle of what seemed to be home brew was nearly empty of liquid, but filled instead by a dark green surprise: a frog. In these parts, various species of back-leaping frogs were used to bring a full-bodied taste to liquor. But even though this lodging house was near the northernmost extreme of the Frontier, it was still difficult for travelers to ignore the local practice. "That right there's the sound of beast weeds blooming. We don't get many dangerous critters in these parts."

Perhaps put at ease by this, the young woman turned from the window and smiled. It was a lonely little smile that suited the seedy lodging house, although the sixteen- or seventeen-year-old brimmed with a beauty that saved her from seeming too gloomy. Even the dreariness of her shirt and slacks, waterproofed with animal fat, were unable to counter the charm lent to her by the silver comb fastened in her red hair.

Out of the collection of five rest houses that made up the unbelievably small community, this was by far the most squalid. There was no one in the brick hall save the innkeeper and three patrons, including the girl. Add two more people, and the room would've been completely packed.

"How far you going anyway, miss?" the innkeeper asked as he turned his liquor bottle upside-down and shook it.

"To Cronenberg," the girl replied.

"Now, I don't know where you hail from, but it's a hell of a thing for a lady like you to choose this of all roads. If you were to take the main road instead, you'd get there a whole lot sooner."

"It'd be a whole lot more dangerous, too. Wouldn't it?" the girl said, covering the leather pouch attached to her belt with the palm of her hand. "The road from the Belhistan region to Cronenberg, in particular, is swarming with monsters. I'd rather not run into any mecha beasts or mazers or any of those types, thank you." Though her tone was colored with loathing, there was no fear in it.

While the back roads that branched off from the main thoroughfares had fewer actual monsters, they were beset by natural disasters such as landslides, quicksand, and impasses, as well as plenty of human monsters—thieves and bandits of all sorts. Traveling alone—especially for a young girl—wasn't something to be undertaken unless you were quite fearless and well trained in the use of weapons. And though the girl's facial features still shone with the innocence of youth, one could catch a glimpse of a resolute will in them as well.

"Well, if you've come this far, there's just a bit further to go—you should be there by tomorrow evening. Get yourself a good night's rest. Fortunately, summer's almost here. The road's pretty rocky, but I suppose the season will make it a touch nicer."

At the innkeeper's appropriately slurred words, the girl got a faraway look in her eye. "Yes, summer," she muttered. "At last."

At that moment, someone beside the reinforced lacquer door said in a hoarse voice, "Florence."

The girl spun around. Surprise tinged her eyes.

"Yes, I thought as much," the voice said with apparent satisfaction.

The girl noticed then that the speaker sat with the electric lantern on his tilting wooden table turned off, melding with the darkness. Despite the fact they were in a house that was all closed up, the man wore a wide-brimmed hat, as well as a woolen cloak. Although the gray hair and beard that hid nearly all of his face testified to his age, the eyes with which he watched the girl brimmed with an uncommon vitality.

"There's no reason to pull such a face," the old man told her. "It's a simple deduction, actually. You have the smell of salt and fish about you, and the comb in your hair is made from the bones of a lion fish, is it not? That's a local specialty. If you grew up in Florence, I'd warrant you have all the pluck you'd need to travel on your own. If you'll pardon my asking, just what manner of business sends you to Cronenberg?"

The old man's eyes gave off a light that seemed to draw her in, and the girl had to turn away.

"Aw, look what you went and did. Now the little lady's all pissed off," the final voice in the room said, rising from another window directly across from the girl. The speaker was a young man, and he'd been the very last to come down from the rooms upstairs. Though his look of fearless determination fit his muscular physique, the pale line running diagonally across his right cheek couldn't help but lend another impression—a less than reputable one.

All present took in the young man's face, but their eyes quickly shifted to his hands. Perhaps the sight of them had stimulated their hearing, for they now heard the sound of the little things sparkling between the fingers of his meaty palms. Squinting her eyes, the girl realized that it was a pair of thin metal rings.

"Care to give it a try?" the man asked, grinning as he held out his right hand to her. The rings were shaking. To the man by the door he said, "You don't ask anyone where they're from or where they're headed—that's the rule of the road. For starters, you haven't even given us your name. I guess as people grow older, they get all inquisitive and such, do they?"

"I wouldn't know," the old man said, shrugging his shoulders. "But I suppose it was impolite of me not to introduce myself. You may call me Professor Krolock. It's not an official title, mind you."

"I'm Wu-Lin," the girl said with a bow. It was an ingrained reaction.

"I'm Toto. Anyway—how about a little wager, missy?" the young man suggested. "It's a simple game, really. All you need to do is separate these two rings. Like so."

Reaching for the loose end with his other hand, the man—Toto—pulled in either direction. The rings came apart without any resistance at all, but no matter how closely Wu-Lin scrutinized where she thought she'd seen them disconnect, she couldn't find any opening or break. Toto quickly put his hands together again, and the rings were back the way they'd been.

"You get three minutes. The bet is for one gold kraken coin."

Wu-Lin's eyes bulged in their sockets. "Those are worth five times their face value on the Frontier," she said in disbelief. "There's no way I'd be carrying that sort of money."

"Good enough. For something else then," Toto said, his smile strangely affable. "What that pretty little hand of yours has been safeguarding the last few minutes."

Startled, Wu-Lin twisted her body to put her waist out of Toto's view, but at the same time two more pairs of eyes concentrated on her from another direction. They were focused on her pouch.

"You're looking awfully pale—must be rather important to you. If it's not cash, I'd say they're jewels . . . or maybe a youth elixir?" And saying that, Toto suddenly got a serious look in his eye again. "Well, if it's all that precious to you, I won't twist your arm. Whatever money you've got will be fine. I'll still put up one kraken coin. And I'm a man of my word."

Wu-Lin's expression shifted. Judging from her wardrobe and her current accommodations, she wasn't exactly traveling in luxury. Kraken coins were produced in extremely limited quantities and were quite valuable. That one coin would be enough for her to hire an armed escort and pay for a carriage all the way to the Capital.

"Relax," the young man said. "Even if I clean you out, I'll at least buy you some breakfast tomorrow morning. Once you've eaten your fill, you'll make it to Cronenberg somehow or other."

His smiling face and equally affable objections served to firm Wu-Lin's resolve. "I paid for my room in advance, but that only leaves me with four coppers," the girl confessed.

"Well, that'll do," Toto said, the silvery rings spinning around his fingertip. "Okay, there's mine."

His left palm went down on the table and then came away again. The glitter of gold colored three pairs of eyes.

Taking a seat in the chair across from him, Wu-Lin lifted the lid of her pouch and thrust her right hand into it. Her left hand kept it covered so no one could see inside. The faces of the four copper coins she produced were covered with a patina.

"That's the spirit!" Toto said. "You get exactly three minutes." Handing the two rings to the girl, he gazed at the magnetic watch around his wrist. "Ready . . . go!"

As he gave the signal, Wu-Lin focused her entire being on the rings in her hands. On closer inspection, one did indeed have a break in it. But while it had an opening, the gap wasn't half as wide as the other ring was thick—it was as thin as a thread. Yet, Toto had gotten them apart. Relying on her memories of what she'd seen, Wu-Lin tried every possible movement with her hands, but the rings remained hopelessly linked.

"Three minutes—time's up!"

As Toto spoke, the girl's shoulders—which were quite solid for someone her age—fell in disappointment. Setting the rings down on the table, she let out a deep sigh.

"I like you, missy," the young man said. "You're not gonna raise a stink and call me a cheat, are you?"

"If I did, would you give me my money back?"

Toto broke into a broad grin. "Sure, why not? I'm not about to give you my coin, but you could walk away with your own. All you'd have to do is give me one itty-bitty peek at what you got in that pouch."

This seemed to be quite a generous offer, and after furrowing her brow for a moment, Wu-Lin soon nodded her agreement. She may have reasoned that because he already knew she was carrying something precious, there was really no point in hiding it. Hers was a rather decisive temperament.

"Hey, you guys better not look. This is just us gamblers squaring away a debt," Toto coldly told the other two men as he watched Wu-Lin's hand disappear into the pouch.

Her hand came right back out. In it was a wad of black velvet. Brusquely setting it down on the table, Wu-Lin pulled the shiny, dark cloth to either side without pretension.

"I see," Toto said, pursing his lips. Rather than being impressed, he seemed a bit suspicious—and more than a tad disappointed.

There lay a semitransparent bead that Wu-Lin could've easily concealed in the palm of her hand. Essentially a sphere, it was marked in places by faint distortions. While the material from which it was crafted was unclear, judging by its dull silver glow, it didn't appear to be any sort of jewel or other precious stone.

"Satisfied?"

"What the hell is it?" Toto asked.

As he reached out with one hand, Wu-Lin quickly jerked the bead away. Carefully re-wrapping it, she said, "It's a kind of pearl."

"It came out of the sea, did it? So, I guess you came all this way to sell it, then. I hate to break it to you, but that thing—"

"It's no concern of yours," Wu-Lin said flatly. Quickly picking up her coppers and putting them and the velvet wad into her pouch, the girl returned to her seat by the window; back to the sound of the wind, and the ever-changing hues of the darkness.

At that moment, there was a dull roar off in the distance—the thunder of hoofbeats. They were drawing closer.

The innkeeper set down the glass he was holding. "No one passes this way at this hour," he said. His voice was stiff.

"It's a traveler," Professor Krolock said, his eyes still shut.

Toto stopped toying with his rings and muttered, "In the dead of night? They'd have to be funny in the head."

No sooner had he spoken than a beastly howl drifted eerily from the opposite direction of the hoofbeats.

"They're out?!" the innkeeper practically screamed as he got to his feet. "It's those damn bronze hounds! They run in packs of ten or so. Can't do squat to 'em with a sword or spear."

"We've got to let whoever it is in!" Wu-Lin said, dashing toward the door, but the innkeeper raced over like the wind and grabbed her tightly.

"Oh, no, you don't," the innkeeper said. "It's too late for that. If those accursed hounds get a whiff of humans, they'll be in here, too!"

"But—" Wu-Lin started to protest, but she caught herself.

The cramped room was filled with the sort of silence that makes the flesh crawl. The sound of the hoofbeats continued to steadily grow louder, and then they seemed to pull aside in front of the door, even though the rider had surely heard the hounds.

A different sound arose from the end of the road: the clatter of countless paws scampering closer.

"We have to help that person!" Wu-Lin swung her foot forcefully, and the innkeeper grabbed his crotch. The girl ran to the door.

"Don't do it!" Toto shouted from behind her, but even as he did, she was reaching for the doorknob.

A split second later, the girl turned right around with her hand still extended and dashed back across the room. Stopping in front of the counter that served as both the bar and the front desk, Wu-Lin was stock-still in amazement, but the rest of the group didn't get to see it. For at that very instant on the other side of the door—right in front of the lodging house—two kinds of footsteps collided, and the night was filled with the howling of beasts.

Wild dogs with hides like blue steel made straight for the poor traveler and his horse. A bladed weapon swung down at the beasts, only to bounce off them in vain. Flesh-rending fangs and blood-spattered muzzles—it was a tragic scene any of them could easily imagine, but a second later it was over. The howls of the bloodthirsty beasts were suddenly cut short, and the thud of one heavy body after another hitting the street echoed out—and then, silence. No, not quite. There was only a hard, faint sound steadily fading in the distance. The sound of hoofbeats.

No one moved, or even said a word.

After a little while, Toto got up and quickly walked over to the door.

"Hey!" the innkeeper called out in voice that was tiny and hoarse. He could imagine what had transpired outside.

Toto roughly threw the door open. The warm nocturnal air was heavy with the scent of fragrant night grasses. The wind struck Toto in the eyes but couldn't tarry there, and the young man caught another of the night's scents.

The moon was out. On the road, the scenery was a stark contrast of black and white. Black seemed to be the stronger of the two.

The smell was coming from a number of pools of blood. The heads and torsos of the bronze-covered wild dogs had already ceased twitching.

"One, two, three—" Toto said, extending a finger with each number. "Exactly ten of the beasts! And all of them put down in less than two seconds—"

Leaping out into the road, Toto gazed in the direction the hoofbeats had gone. The howls of the night wind made his well-trimmed hair and the hem of his coat billow in the same direction.

"It might've been *him* . . ." the others in the doorway heard Toto mutter as he faced the darkness that swallowed the end of the road. "He can travel by night. And all alone."

II

Early the next morning, Wu-Lin left the lodging house; she didn't even bother to eat. The innkeeper and the other guests were still asleep, and the eastern sky was just beginning to shine with a watery light. Dressed in the same clothes as the night before, she was shouldering a vinyl backpack.

Three minutes' walk brought the girl to the edge of town. Beyond the fence, a cedar so huge it would take three men to get their arms around it stretched up to the blue sky. In this region, it was customary to grow enormous trees on either side of the main road through town. It was hoped that doing so would bring the community some of the same mysterious vitality the trees possessed. Past the massive cedar, the rows of trees continued.

Opening the gate and then shutting it again behind herself, the girl was just about to walk off when someone appeared from behind the foliage.

"Professor Krolock?" Wu-Lin said.

A gray-haired head bobbed at the receiving end of her tense gaze.

"Good morning, young lady. Off to an early start, I see." Placing one hand on his chest, the professor bowed elegantly.

"So are you," Wu-Lin replied. "I wouldn't have thought you'd be out before me."

"Actually, I couldn't get much sleep. At any rate, if it pleases you, would you accompany me to Cronenberg?"

"Are you headed there too, Professor?"

"Actually," the old man said, "I am. My carriage is parked behind yonder tree."

"You sure I wouldn't be intruding?" Wu-Lin said, staring intently at him in his scarlet cloak.

"Whatever could you possibly mean?"

"Why ask me way out here?" the girl inquired.

"I might've suggested it back at the lodging house, but there was a certain boisterous individual around."

"And you wanted me all to yourself?" asked Wu-Lin.

"Precisely," the old man replied, a smile forming on his lips. "Approaching you in town was going to be troublesome, so I simply waited out here. I wouldn't be so cruel as to say I don't care what happens to a young lady like yourself. Please, join me. All I ask in payment is that bead you have in your possession."

"I thought as much. I guess it's a good thing I showed it off so no one got too curious and slit my throat while I slept." Wu-Lin asked the old man, "Do you know what it's worth?"

"Probably better than that rabble last night," the professor said, closing his eyes and nodding to himself. "But, as yet, I don't have a good idea of its true value. To really ascertain as much, I'd need you to hand it over to me."

"Sorry. I travel alone." As if in jest, the girl bowed exactly as the professor had, and then a second later she sprinted off like the wind.

Not bothering to chase after the girl as she swiftly dwindled in the distance, the professor muttered, "Such a tempestuous child," and thrust both hands into his cloak. What they came out with were very strange items indeed. His right hand held a quill pen, and his left hand held a brownish scrap of paper—or rather, a dried piece of animal hide.

Returning to the tree and leaning against it, he raised his right hand. Without seeming to particularly steel himself for the task, he took the sharp tip of the pen and stabbed it into his left wrist. Not even glancing at the gore that spread across his skin when he pulled it out again, he took the blood-dipped pen and began to draw something on the surface of the parchment—what looked to be a human face. After about ten seconds, the pen's movements ceased. Running his eyes over his handiwork at length and nodding with satisfaction, the professor then embarked on an even stranger course of action. Lovingly bringing his face closer to the portrait of darkening red, he began to whisper something in a low voice.

Having already run more than a hundred yards, the girl suddenly found her feet getting heavier. A hue of bewilderment rose in her face. While she didn't stop, she had noticed a rather odd phenomenon—her legs seemed to be gradually losing their strength, to the point where she couldn't run any longer.

"I—why is this happening . . ." With those weary words, Wu-Lin squatted down right then and there.

Less than a minute later, a wagon drawn by a pair of cyborg horses rumbled along with a sound that hardly suited a road at daybreak, stopping right behind the girl as she crouched down, cradling her knees. It went without saying that the man who sat in the driver's seat holding a whip was Professor Krolock. The grotesque parchment was rolled up in his left hand.

From his lofty perch, the professor said, "You mustn't keep these problems to yourself. I'll be happy to hear them. Won't you climb into my carriage, so the two of us might mull over your dilemma? Come."

All exaggeration aside, the old man's tone truly swam with affection. At the sound of his voice, Wu-Lin got up and began to walk toward the wagon without the slightest hesitation.

And then something equally bizarre occurred. The professor's right hand abruptly shot out, and with a sharp crack from his whip, the wagon made a wide turn toward town—back the way they'd come. Odd as it may seem, the same professor who'd taken the trouble to follow Wu-Lin then cracked the whip again and, scattering fragments of the dawn's light like so much dust and ice, started off in the opposite direction in a great hurry.

As the old man and his wagon vanished down the road, another figure stepped out from behind the trees that towered by the roadside and into view of the paralyzed Wu-Lin. He was leading a horse. His right hand was clearly toying with a pair of gold rings that kept clinking together.

Waving his left hand before the eyes of the mesmerized Wu-Lin, the mysterious young traveler—Toto—made a wry face. "He calls himself a man of learning, and then he goes and puts some weird spell on a girl like you—that's really tempting the wrath of heaven. That said, I must confess I'm after the same thing myself. Don't take it too hard," he told the girl. "Looks like I was right when I guessed that bead was really something after all. Allow me to be of some assistance."

Wu-Lin seemed to have had the very soul drained out of her, and at this point a baby probably could've taken what it wanted from her. Tapping her pale cheek with his right hand as if humoring her, the man was reaching for her pouch with his left hand when something hot whizzed right by the end of his nose.

"There she is!"

"Don't let her get away!"

Not only could a cacophony of shouts and hoofbeats be heard coming from the direction of town, but the sharp whistles that came from the figures closing on the pair soon became steel arrows in flight.

"Just as I thought—company! And here that old innkeeper was trying to come off so friendly and all. The world's a nasty place. Sorry, but this is where I make my exit," Toto said.

But as the young man's hand reached once more for the pouch, it was caught by Wu-Lin's. Just as the shock was re-coloring Toto's complexion, his wrist was expertly twisted back against the joint and the man was physically thrown a good ten feet down the road. And yet, the way he executed a skillful one-hundred-eighty-degree roll and landed lightly on his feet was truly an eye-opening display of acrobatics.

"Hey! Wait just a second!" Toto shouted, but just as he was about to charge back to the girl, a number of arrows flew over his head. As he hit the ground despite himself, the sound of iron-shod hooves and excited shouts reached his ears.

A shadowy form leapt over his head. Needless to say, the rider holding the reins of Toto's cyborg horse was none other than Wu-Lin.

"Thanks for the horse. See you!" With that brief shout, the girl, who'd escaped from the professor's spell before Toto even caught on, slammed her right heel into the mount's flank and galloped away as fast as she could.

Riding for a full hour at breakneck speed, Wu-Lin was a few miles from an intersection with the main road in an area still lit with the cold, clear rays of dawn before she finally let her horse rest its legs. At any rate, she was probably safe for the moment. She never would've thought those two men would be lying in wait for her, and it'd certainly been a mistake to fall under that mysterious spell, but since she'd managed to extricate herself from the situation, none of that mattered anymore. Having acquired a horse in the bargain, it was likely she'd reach Cronenberg at just past noon instead of in the evening.

Recalling the stunned look on Toto's face as she'd thrown him, Wu-Lin smiled innocently, but it took less than two seconds for that smile to freeze. The sound of hoofbeats was again growing nearer.

She thought it might be the "professor," but there was no squeak of wagon wheels. What she saw were a number of horses—and racers, at that. They wouldn't be out delivering mail at this hour. Was it the last group that'd shown up as she was leaving?

Just as Wu-Lin was about to give a kick to her mount's flanks, something whistled through the air as it dropped toward her. Sparks shot up on the right half of the road about ten feet ahead of her, and a fierce shock wave knocked both horse and rider down on their sides. It was the work of a portable firebomb launcher. An expert could hit a target the size of a brick from over two hundred yards away, but if they were only trying to blow something up, all they had to do was increase the amount of gunpowder.

Wu-Lin immediately got up. For the time being, her foes were only trying to slow her down, and fortunately for her, they seemed to be concerned about damaging the bead and had adjusted the amount of gunpowder accordingly. As a result, the girl hadn't been fatally wounded, or even broken a single bone.

As Wu-Lin tried to get her horse back on its feet, she coughed— the urge to vomit was building within her. In truth, she'd taken a blow to the stomach when she fell. Jamming a finger down her throat, she retched immediately. As she vomited, she realized her horse was a lost cause—its neck was twisted grotesquely. If it had been one of the models cherished by the Nobility, it would've continued to run even if the entire head had been torn off, but this one was intended for humans. Wiping her lips, Wu-Lin shouldered her bag and looked around. The woods were thick to either side. Behind her, the silhouettes of riders formed hazily in the white light. She couldn't afford to hesitate.

Wu-Lin ran to the right—the woods might serve to restrict the movements of horses. The trees and bushes would probably provide her with some cover from the explosives as well.

Just when she thought she'd melted into the grove of the trees, an impact slammed into her from behind, and a sharp pain shot through her back—probably a branch or a small stone. The next thing she knew, she was lying on the ground. Putting all of her strength into her limbs, she tried to get up.

Right behind her she heard a familiar voice say, "Give up already. We'll make it quick for you." It was the innkeeper.

Wu-Lin got to her feet without looking in his direction. About five yards ahead of her was a thick grove. *How many seconds would it take me to get there?* she wondered.

"We don't wanna blow that doodad of yours to kingdom come, you know. So we won't finish you with the mortar. What do you fancy, a sword or an arrow? Or would you prefer we garrote you?"

More voices than she could count laughed in unison.

Wu-Lin started to make a break for it, and then stopped. At the same time, the laughter dwindled as well.

Why is everyone always popping out from behind trees? Wu-Lin wondered.

The newest arrival was a dashing figure. He wore a wide-brimmed traveler's hat and a black long coat that sheathed his tall form elegantly. The longsword on his back had a graceful curve to it. For a second, Wu-Lin had to wonder whether it wasn't a moonlit night at present. But the reason she and the men behind her froze was because they unconsciously knew that an aura of extreme danger lingered around the gorgeous stranger.

"Who the hell are you?!" someone asked, his voice quavering.

Wu-Lin swiftly circled around behind the figure's back. "Help me!" she cried. "They're bandits!"

The stranger didn't move.

"Out of the way, pretty boy," the innkeeper said.

There were half a dozen men on horseback, with the innkeeper leading the pack, and all of them wore vicious scowls. Surely their racket consisted of finding travelers with something valuable, then following them when they left and killing them. They were armed with swords and spears, but the man to the far right was the only one with disk-shaped bombs loaded into a crossbow-like launcher pointed at the ground.

"Well, it doesn't really matter," the innkeeper said to the huge fellow to his right. "Now that he's seen our faces, it's not like we're about to let him live. We'll send him to his reward along with the girl." To the pair he added, "Just consider this your brief romance, and kiss each other goodbye!"

As she listened to his cruel words, Wu-Lin clung tightly to the back of the shadowy figure. But something suddenly became apparent. The man in black wasn't looking at the other men. At the end of his gaze was a grove of trees and sparkling green leaves. Between him and the other men faint beams of light swayed— sunlight peeking through the trees. Wu-Lin looked up at his profile—there wasn't a hint of sadness on his face. It put Wu-Lin's heart at ease.

Broadswords and spears glittered in the men's hands. With wild shouts, they charged the stranger.

Still, Wu-Lin remained entranced, enchanted by the beauty of this strange young man.

Hammering the earth beneath them, a pair of riders raced by the stranger—one on either side—and kept right on riding, with blood

streaming out behind them. From the waist up, the riders no longer existed. Before the rest of the killers realized what had happened, the upper bodies of their compatriots were lying at the shadowy figure's feet. Bloody mists tinged the white sunlight.

When the startled man with the launcher readied his weapon, the figure kicked off the ground without a sound. The hem of his coat flickered like a dream.

A head flew. The innkeeper's torso fell in two distinct pieces.

Seeing what looked like the figure's chest being penetrated by spears thrust from either side, Wu-Lin cried out. But the shadowy figure was in midair now. What the murderous implements had pierced was merely his afterimage.

A circular flash slashed through the necks of the last two men. When the figure landed on the ground again, there was one more flash of light as he flung the gore from his blade onto the green grass, and then the weapon returned to the sheath on his back. A head landed on the ground far off, and the rest of the body dropped off at the horse's feet.

The massacre had unfolded in the time it took to blink.

Dazed, Wu-Lin rubbed her eyes. The images she observed weren't the least bit ghastly. The sunlit scene of carnage was like some shadow-puppet show.

It's his fault, she thought fuzzily. *He's so beautiful; he even makes death look good.*

The shadowy figure returned. His footsteps made no sound at all; he could walk across water without making a ripple. He was a young man. That was all she knew. The cool mood the tall man in black seemed to generate didn't allow the girl to return to her senses until he was in the middle of putting a saddle onto a cyborg horse that was tethered to a tree not far away.

Wu-Lin ran over to the stranger in spite of herself and bowed. "Thank you," she said. "You saved my life."

As the young man loaded what looked to be a sleeping bag behind his saddle, he asked, "Are you on foot?"

Perhaps any other information about the girl or the circumstances surrounding that deadly battle didn't matter. They had attacked him, and he cut them down. Brutal as it was, that was a perfectly natural way to live on the Frontier.

"Yes," the girl replied.

"Use one of their horses."

"Um—" Wu-Lin stammered, but before she could say anything more, the man in black was on his mount. "Are you going with me?" she finally managed to say, but her words struck the stranger's broad back as he'd already ridden a few paces.

"I'm looking for somewhere to get some sleep."

Wu-Lin didn't understand his reply at all. The world was swimming in light.

"At least tell me your name. I'm Wu-Lin," the girl called out, her shouts blocked by the grove.

And then a reply came from the very same stand of trees: "D."

III

Cronenberg was a town that stretched across the plains one hundred and twenty miles north of the center of the Frontier. This small city, with its population of thirty thousand, was a far cry from the scale of the Capital, but as a place where goods were collected from all over the Frontier it kept the roads well-repaired, and the community maintained a decent level of activity all year round. They maintained cold storage for seafood shipped from the coast, vast processing plants for livestock that grazed on the plains, drying houses for vegetables and grains—and for the rest and relaxation of those involved in the transportation of all these things and the guards that kept them safe from bandits and beasts, there were saloons and hotels, casinos, and women.

The chatter of men and women persisted all day long in the area where the drinking establishments could be found, but once dusk settled like a thin wash of ink, the multicolored lights grew brighter and the strides of people on the streets got lighter. As the number of monsters and supernatural beasts in this plains region was comparatively low, the streets were never empty from evening to the wee hours of the morning.

It was at twilight that Wu-Lin arrived at the settlement. The cyborg horse she rode was one that'd belonged to the thugs D had killed in the woods. Asking one of the guards about a certain shop as he opened the gate for her, Wu-Lin then proceeded to the center of town.

While it wasn't especially uncommon for a woman to travel alone, it still came as little surprise that the remarkably untamed beauty of the girl's face and body drew the eyes of men on the street.

It was in front of a tiny little shop that Wu-Lin dismounted. The sign bore the words "Cyrus's Curio Shop" painted in letters that were now almost completely blurred. Tethering her horse's reins to a pole outside, Wu-Lin went into the shop.

The dusty odor of old furniture reached her nose. Old-fashioned tables and chairs, paintings, sculptures, antique mirrors—the merchandise that rested in the murky light differed little from what would be found in any such shop, but that wasn't why Wu-Lin was there. When she struck the call bell that sat on the counter in the back, a door that looked to be something of an antique itself opened, and a middle-aged man who was little more than skin and bones appeared.

"Welcome," the man said as he ran his eyes over Wu-Lin.

"There's something I'd like you to have a look at," Wu-Lin said, covering her pouch with one hand.

"Well, that's the line of work I'm in, so I guess I'll take a gander," the man replied in a less-than-amiable tone. "But unless it's something really spectacular, you won't get much for it from me. Especially not for curios—"

"It's not old."

"No?" the man remarked. "So you want an appraisal, then?"

"Yes."

Dubiously eyeing the package Wu-Lin opened in her hand, the man picked up the sphere. "What is it?" he asked.

"I don't know. That's why I'm here."

Shrugging his shoulders, the man then held the sphere up to his eye. "Where did you come by it?"

"Near my house. On the beach there."

The man's eyes shifted for a second to Wu-Lin. "From the sea?" he muttered. "You know, I can't tell much without really looking into it. Would it be okay if I kept it?"

"How long?"

"Let me see—till noon tomorrow."

"Could you write me up a receipt for it?" asked the girl.

"Sure."

Taking a form imprinted with the proper information from behind the counter, the man hastily signed it and handed it to Wu-Lin.

"Whereabouts are you staying?"

"I haven't decided yet," the girl replied. "I'll be back again at noon."

Pointing down the street, the man said, "Take a right down at the corner and you'll find a hotel. Quarters are cramped, but it's cheap and the service is good."

"Thank you," Wu-Lin said with a smile as she turned to leave.

Making sure she'd gone, the man went into the back room and set the sphere on the desk he used for appraising antiques. Taking a seat, he didn't use any of the electronic lenses or microscopes around him, but rather rolled the sphere around in his hand. Suddenly seeming to recall something, he looked up and smacked his fist to his forehead. Several minutes passed before the following words spilled from his lips: "So that's it . . . I remember now! I'm sure it was in that book . . . This is a Noble's . . ."

As the blood drained from his already corpse-like countenance, the man grabbed his jacket from the back of another chair, stashed the sphere in his pocket, and headed for the door with lengthy strides. What the man didn't notice as he reached for the doorknob was that his body had turned in entirely the opposite direction.

With the same tense expression as ever on his face, he walked toward the window on the far side of the room with a much gentler gait.

The door opened behind him. And who should step in but Toto, cautiously surveying the room as he entered. Judging from the way he quickly walked over to the man and fished the sphere out of his pocket, he must've seen everything the shopkeeper had done since entering the back room. Giving a light tap on the shoulder of the man who thought he was still facing the door, the mysterious young gentleman bounced the bead from his right hand and the pair of rings from his left in the palm of his hand. "Sorry," he told the shopkeeper, "but I'll be taking this. Kindly give my regards to the little lady. See you!"

With these words, Toto took off like a gust of wind. But even after he was gone, the owner of the curio shop just kept plodding slowly toward the window—although in his own mind, he was hurrying toward the door.

About an hour later, several men went into a saloon with the gaudiest neon sign of all the drinking establishments that lined the bustling thoroughfare. Their fierce eyes, expressions, and powerful bodies made it quite evident they were in a dangerous line of work. Heading straight to the counter in the back, one of them said something to the bartender, who then used the hand that'd been wiping out glasses to indicate a door far to the right.

"That little bastard—you've gotta be joking me," spat the man who'd spoken to the bartender, curses rolling from his lips like an incantation. When he tossed his jaw in the direction of the door, the other men started across the room with a brutal wind in their wake. A pair of muscular brutes who looked like bodyguards stood by the door, one on either side, but they let the group pass without saying a word.

Just beyond the door lay a hallway with a row of garish pink doors on the green wall. Though no voices or other sounds could be heard, the men knew what was going on behind the bright-pink planks, and it seemed like they could almost see the hot, dense fog rising from each and every door. Out on the Frontier, it wasn't at all rare for saloons to double as whorehouses.

Stopping for a second, they checked the number plate above one of the doors, and then the whole group headed down the hall to the right. The door down by the first corner was their destination.

When they were a few steps shy of their goal, they all heard a woman's voice shout, "What are you doing?! I told you I'm not going for that, you lousy pervert!" At the same time, the door swung open from the inside. Along with the sweet smell of spices, something pale flew from the room: a half-naked woman. She clutched her clothes to the front of her body.

"You bastard!" the woman shouted. Her sensuous face twisted into a demonic visage, and she swung her right hand. Something shot back into the room; there was a dull thud and then a cry of pain.

"Take that, you fucking deviant!" the woman roared before she growled to the group, "Out of my way!"

While watching the woman stalk away indignantly, the men grinned at each other and then heard someone say, "Damn, that hurt! Where'd you run off to, bitch?!"

Spewing curses and groans all the while, a powerful form clad only in a pair of briefs appeared. His right hand was pressed against his forehead, and he had a high-heeled shoe dangling loosely from his left. A pendant of two interlocked rings swayed against his hairy, muscular chest.

"I paid you a good chunk of change. The least you could do is indulge me a little! I'll grab your sorry ass and—" At that point, he noticed the men and said, "What the hell do you want?"

"Been a long time, hasn't it, Toto?" the man who'd spoken with the bartender said with nostalgia . . . only his eyes weren't smiling.

Staring intently at his face, Toto broke into a nostalgic grin, too. "Well, spank my ass if it ain't Peres! This is some coincidence. You still doing the roving bodyguard routine?"

"Looks like neither of us has changed," Peres replied. "When I heard about what happened at the antique store, I knew it was you. Seems you're as good as ever with that trick of yours."

Toto was playing down his abilities as he reached for his chest, but his pendant jolted away right before his hand.

Staring thoughtfully at the rings he'd torn free, Peres forcefully suggested, "Let's talk inside."

Still rubbing the back of his neck, Toto replied, "First, I have to get that bitch and—"

But as he attempted to go out into the hall, there was a dull thud against his solar plexus. Doubling over with a groan, he was roughly shoved back inside by the man who'd just punched him.

As he fell in the center of the medium-sized room, Toto groaned, "What the hell . . . was that about?" His Adam's apple bobbed madly as he tried to take a breath.

"Check his clothes," Peres ordered one of his compatriots as he bent over Toto.

The room had no decorations, save a bed and an end table—Toto's clothes had been strewn on top of the table. Above the wall that the bed was attached to, a glass window reflected the neon lights outside.

"You stuck your nose in a hell of a place this time," Peres said in a sinister tone. His eyes were laughing. "Though I don't figure you ever dreamed things would go like this. Without me around, Mr. Gilligan wouldn't have ever known about you, or the fact that you like this place more than three hots and a cot. Too bad, eh?"

"Who the hell is *that*?" Toto asked in a tone that was somehow calm. Apparently his pain had subsided.

"Why, he's the big boss who runs everything here in town. That was a serious mistake, making a move on a curio shop he's connected to. I hear there's something unbelievable all tied into this. The boss went completely nuts and had us grab not just you, but the girl who brought it here to have it looked at. Hey, now," Peres cautioned Toto, "don't try and slip away. I know all your tricks. I know how tough you are, too, but these guys do this for a living. You don't want them taking you apart alive, I bet."

Having said his piece, Peres then turned toward the end table.

"It's not here," said the man searching through Toto's clothes. "Where'd you stash it? Your hotel?"

"Yeah," Toto replied with a pained nod.

"All right, then. We'll all go get it. But I'm warning you—if I find out you're jerking us off to buy some time . . ." Peres said, lifting the corner of his coat. A sheath with a broadsword hung against his leg. They were convenient items, and depending on what your needs were, they could be used for anything from butchering a fire dragon to skinning a man alive.

"Do whatever you like," Toto said as he stood up.

"Give him back his clothes," Peres told his compatriot, adding, "But only after you've torn all the pockets out."

A few seconds later Toto's garments were thrown back to him, and he quickly put them on. "What happened to the girl?" he asked.

"You worried about her?"

"Yeah. I know what a scumbag you are and how you like to get your kicks. You don't exactly take it easy on women or children, do you?"

"You'll just have to wait till we're in Mr. Gilligan's basement to see about that, I guess."

"Fine with me," Toto said, his body sinking.

Catching a vicious shoulder attack in the stomach, Peres flew toward the table.

"You little bastard!" the other men snarled, although the reason they all charged Toto immediately must've been because they knew he was unarmed. Perhaps that was all they had in mind as they attacked.

A metallic *clink!* rang out.

Peres watched in a daze as his compatriots completely ignored their forward momentum and sharply turned around a mere foot shy of Toto.

"Where the hell did you have 'em?!" he shouted as his right hand raced to his broadsword, but his eyes then went wide with a second surprise.

"Right here!"

The flash of silver that shot forth with Toto's words answered both of Peres's questions simultaneously.

Hacking half-way through the man's neck with his own blade, Toto spit something out of his mouth for the other man to see just as his old acquaintance fell to the floor gushing blood: a pair of metal rings.

"Never showed you that before, did I? Don't go thinking things never change," Toto lectured Peres, whose head flopped to one side. He then dashed over to the window, threw it open, and leapt out.

He landed on the street along the left side of the saloon—the moon was now out. Crouching down, he ran. To the rear there was a cluster of eateries. Avoiding them, he quickly turned right instead. The alley was murky. If he kept going straight, he'd come out at the grain storehouses.

As he put his strength into his legs, a crisp sound reverberated behind him. Whistling. Toto became a statue—it had that sort of ring to it. Nevertheless, Toto managed to slowly turn around.

At the entrance to the alley he'd just gone into, a figure in blue stood illuminated by the moonlight. He was tall and wore a cape. A sword hung from his left hip, and the handle and sheath were both covered with exquisitely intricate carvings. Both hands wore leather gloves, and they hung naturally by his sides. And yet, it was perfectly clear that they would flash into action in response to any slight movement. Occasionally you encountered people like this. Perhaps he was one of the men after Toto, waiting outside as a precaution?

"What do you want with me?" Toto called out, his tone surprisingly calm. Surely he hadn't exactly led a normal, peaceful existence, either. "Are you with them?"

"Come with me," a gorgeous voice said. It was as clear and fresh as the moonlight.

"What for?"

"Because you're the suspicious character I saw break open a window and run away. I'm taking you to the sheriff's office."

"Spare me. C'mon, pal. From the look of you, you're not more than a step or two out of my world yourself. As a favor to another guy, just let me go, okay?"

His reply: a whistle.

A certain feeling suddenly filled Toto's heart. It was that sort of melody. And the instant it completely filled his ears, a flash of white mowed through Toto's abdomen, and his body was blasted by a lust for killing.

Toto somehow managed to jump. However, as he hung in the air, blood spread from him like smoke. When he landed fifteen feet away, a grotesque mass of intestines spilled from his belly with a gush of blackish blood.

Toto couldn't believe it. The distance between him and the man with the drawn blade in his right hand had to have been fifteen feet *at the very least*. Now, there was less than six feet between them. How had his opponent closed the other nine feet?

Something hot welled up within him, and no longer able to bear it, he coughed. More than just gore splashed out in the alley. Even covered with dark blood, the sphere retained its dull shine as it bounced once on the ground and then gingerly rolled across the alley.

Just behind the bead, Toto finally noticed the other alley to his right that lay wide open. However, that new path wasn't to be his escape route. Pinning him to the ground with the sheer ferocity of his will to kill, the gorgeous man calmly drew closer with his naked blade. There was no doubt in Toto's mind that any movement now would only invite a deadly blow. With desperate eyes, he gazed down at the puddle of blood at his feet—the pair of interlocked rings was in there somewhere. He heard whistling. When it stopped, the moment of fate would come. The melody flowed on—then faded away. The blood seemed to drain from every inch of Toto. And then . . . nothing.

Toto looked up at his foe, but his opponent wasn't looking at him.
His gaze was concentrated on another alley.

Following the other man's eyes, Toto found it was now his turn to
be astonished. There before him was a man's face so gorgeous it could
make even someone caught in hellish agony lose himself. He saw
something darker than any ordinary darkness—a darkness given
human form that hovered at the entrance to the alley. A vision of
beauty. That was the only way he could describe it. The face beneath
the traveler's hat melded with the darkness, but had he been able to
actually see it, the sight might've left him breathless with sheer envy.
Perhaps it was some spell that the night put on him that caused these
two gorgeous men to appear before him in that narrow alleyway.

The second figure bent over and picked up the bead. He left himself
so wide open to attack that it looked like a mere child could cut
him down. Gazing at the bead, he asked, "Is this yours?"

"Yes, I'm sorry to say," Toto replied. And as he spoke, he took
the intestines lying in the road and began stuffing them back
into his abdominal cavity. "See, someone gave it to me. You
know, I hate to do this, but I have a favor to ask of you. I have
to be running along now, but I was hoping you could help out the
bead's owner. And I'll let you keep that as payment. Seems it's
really worth a hell of a lot. Although I do have to warn you,
I'll be along later to take it back. You'll find her in the basement
of a scumbag by the name of Gilligan. I'm counting on you, pal."

With these words, Toto leapt away to the rear. While it wasn't
clear exactly what the secret of his physiology was, his strength was
unbelievable. The whistling figure didn't follow him.

"What will you do?" he said. It sounded as if the moon had asked
the question.

There was no reply.

"You plan on going?"

"We'll see," the new arrival said, responding for the first time.

The whistling figure continued, "You're even better looking than
I am—never met a man like that before. What's more, I believe I

know your name. Vampire Hunter D. I may as well introduce myself. The name is Glen. I'm a seeker of knowledge."

He received no reply.

"Once again, I'd like to know if you intend to go or not."

D's outline melted into the darkness.

Glen looked up at the sky. Dark clouds were blindfolding the moon. They then cleared, but there was no sign of D.

"I guess you went," Glen muttered in a low voice.

After a while, the melancholy whistling faded off in the moonlit distance.

Message from the Departed

CHAPTER 2

I

Wu-Lin slowly realized what was happening to her—staying at the hotel the curio dealer had told her about had proved to be her undoing. Ordinarily, she'd have made a conscious effort to avoid such a place. But she was exhausted at the time, and also greatly relieved to have entrusted the bead to someone else. Checking into the cheapest room they had, she'd quickly taken a bath, and then stood before the mirror.

No one had ever told her she was pretty before. Personally, she thought her face and body were quite plain. She didn't ordinarily wear makeup, either. Life on the northern coast really didn't allow for such things. Her fingers grazed her own face. *It's so rough*, she thought. The wind off the sea was cold, and it carried grains of salt that bit into her skin like tiny shards of glass. And though she might try to fend it off, the wind always kept lashing away at her with those frosty particles whenever it blew. Somewhere along the line she'd forgotten all about wiping the salt off. She opened both hands, and with the fingers of her left she brushed the palm of her right. So tough. It felt like the whole thing was made up of nothing but calluses. Even the tips of the fingers she touched to it were hardened.

At around the age of three she'd started gathering shellfish. When she'd touched the razor-like shells, a sharp pain had shot through her as her tender young flesh was split with consummate ease. When she burst into tears, her mother had taken her hands and held them in the briny sea, saying, "This is just how your sister and I always took care of it." In no time, the mollusks gave way to fish, and shells were replaced by scales as sharp as knives. As always, the blood gushed from her, and Wu-Lin stuck her hands into the salty sea without hesitation.

Sixteen years had passed. But today was the first time Wu-Lin had ever been ashamed of her sun-baked skin and rough hands—this morning, to be more precise. In the sun-dappled woods, a young man in black had danced with a bloody breeze. So beautiful it gave her goose bumps, his staggeringly sad visage had stirred something in her chest. He'd said his name was D.

Going over to the bed, Wu-Lin pulled out the backpack she'd hidden beneath it. Opening a leather flap, she inspected her clothes. All she had was another blouse and a change of underwear. The top was clean, but it had been patched in spots. Though sturdy, its color had faded. After putting on the fresh blouse and a pair of pants, she stood before the mirror.

Why didn't I bring a skirt? she thought. *At least that would've hidden these fat legs of mine. The one with the white flower print would make me look a little prettier.*

But whom would she want to look so nice for? A gorgeous young man who wavered on the thin line between life and death with his emotionless swordplay. D.

Wu-Lin again rubbed her cheeks. Just then, she heard a sound at the door. The instant she turned to see a human shape, something warm slammed into her solar plexus and her consciousness sank into darkness. The next thing she knew, she was somewhere else entirely. With stone walls on all sides, the room seemed to be a basement of some sort—the ceiling was lit by electric lights. Her surroundings were painfully clear, and fear gushed from every pore on her. Wu-Lin was chained hand and foot to the stone wall. All along the wall hung those who'd suffered similar fates, now skeletons clad only in rags. Even more lay on the floor below the chains.

Wu-Lin let out a scream. And another, and another. Her every struggle sent her shackles biting into her wrists and ankles, where they tore ruthlessly at her flesh. She didn't even notice the sound of a door opening somewhere.

Before Wu-Lin knew it, there was someone standing right before her—three people, actually. The ones to either side were clearly bodyguards by the look of them, but their boss in the middle was somewhat odd. His seven-hundred-pound frame was surrounded by a steel cage. Clothed in the largest three-piece suit imaginable, he lay on his side against the floor of the cage that held him a good three feet off the ground. He was like a slug that'd sprouted arms and legs. His face looked pushed in, and his pitifully sparse hair was parted to one side. With no neck to speak of, his head seemed to be melded right into his torso. The black stub stuck between his thick lips must've been a cigar. His eyes were thin as a thread, and his nostrils and mouth spread wide to either side. In fact, he was so hideously misshapen, he looked like a human that'd been given a frog's head.

It had finally dawned on Wu-Lin that the cage around him—steel rings running horizontally and vertically—was not actually intended as a prison, but rather served to support his body. Each of the rings was jointed, and they twisted subtly to prop up the listing seven-hundred-pound frame. What's more, the part of the device that made contact with the floor seemed to be some sort of walker.

"Nice to meet you, miss," the clothed blob of flesh said. His voice was so shrill and nauseating it made the girl want to plug her ears. "I'm Gilligan. And I happen to have the pleasure of running this town. I had you brought here because there are a few little things I'd like to ask you about."

"Let me out of here. And get these chains off of me while you're at it."

"There, there. If you'll talk to me, we can do that soon enough. I suppose you'd like to know why I'd subject a pretty young lady like yourself to this sort of treatment. Well, it's because this way will get you to tell me the whole truth faster."

"What do you want to know?"

"For starters, I'd like to know a little something about the bead you brought to the curio shop. Where and how did you happen to get it?"

Wu-Lin's eyes went wide with astonishment. Speared now by a far greater sense of hopelessness about her fate, the girl slumped against her chains. "You mean to tell me the guy that runs that shop . . ."

"There, there, my child. He and I have a little arrangement. Once or twice a year some clown will bring in something quite valuable without having the slightest clue about what they have. The deal is that the shopkeeper lets me know about it, and I buy said item for a reasonable price."

"Give it back. I want it back right now."

"I don't happen to have it at the moment—you see, it was stolen," Gilligan said, raising a horrendously short and fat hand to scratch his head. The plump appendage had the form of a child's but was three times the size of an adult's. As he moved, the ring that supported his arm creaked. He had only to put the slightest pressure on a joint, and the rings would then move his limb in that same direction. Without that bizarre contraption, he most likely wouldn't be able to so much as lift a finger. Moreover, it was perfectly clear that if gravity were allowed to have its way with that great mound of flesh and fat, a horrifying death would await the man as all his internal organs were crushed by his own weight.

"Who in the world took it?"

Seeing the urgency in Wu-Lin's expression, Gilligan laughed raspily. Even his own bodyguards looked unsettled by the sound of it. "Relax. We know who the thief was and where he is, and some of my people are on their way to collect the item. They should be back presently with both it and the culprit. But while I'm waiting, I need you to tell me a few things."

"I don't know anything at all. I don't know anything about the bead."

"You expect me to believe that some clueless little girl is running around with something like that?!"

Wu-Lin gnawed her lip. Her lovely countenance was imbued with a look of firm resistance.

"The Nobility," Gilligan said out of the blue.

Wu-Lin's expression wavered for a moment and then quickly returned to normal. But not quickly enough.

"See, I was certain you knew something about it. Well, now, this is starting to get amusing." Moving both hands with what seemed to be a great effort, the human slug clapped them together before his own chest. In addition to the grinding gears of the joints, a revolting sound like a shellfish being cracked open shook the air.

"There's no point in asking me anything about it, you know. There's nothing I can tell you."

Watching with a sort of lust in his eyes as Wu-Lin turned her face away from him, Gilligan said, "Good enough. You don't have to if you don't want to. I'm afraid you have me all wrong, Miss. I'm not asking you to tell me anything you don't want to. To the contrary— it's all the more enjoyable if you won't tell me."

Wu-Lin's eyes went wide. There was a cruelty to the words of this mysterious man that shook her to the core. "What are you going to do?" she asked, the question pushed out by her fear.

"Are you in such a hurry to learn your fate?" Gilligan asked, holding the cigar out in front of himself with one hand. Clanking all the while, the legs went into action, carrying him to a spot on the floor less than three feet from Wu-Lin before they stopped. "Okay. I'll show you then."

Gilligan flicked the cigar with his fingers. Wu-Lin gasped, although it was almost a laugh. It wasn't a cigar. The jet black stub twisted and unfolded, forming a longer creature that began creeping toward her feet. Like an inchworm, it folded and straightened its body, and on its head it had a pair of strangely oversized simple eyes and a thorn-like proboscis for a mouth.

"That nasty little insect is what's known as a 'chatterbug.' When one bites you, you can't help but tell the truth," Gilligan said, licking his lips.

"No, not that!" Wu-Lin cried, writhing. Countless beads of sweat streamed down her face, neck, and back. A single droplet from her wildly shaking face fell on the insect's head, causing the unearthly creature to rear back in surprise. But in the blink of an eye it started forward again. It reached her feet, and then it climbed up on her shoe. She tried to kick it off, but only ended up making the shackles gouge deeper into the meat of her leg.

"Stop!"

Crawling across the girl's ankle, it brushed the cuff of her pants.

"Stop it!"

It started to climb up the outside of her clothes.

"Stop it! Just stop it!"

It reached her blouse and kept climbing. The girl's face was reflected in the insect's dim black eyes all the while. And its sharp proboscis chirped incessantly.

"Don't!" Wu-Lin screamed, thrashing her head back and forth like a woman possessed.

As the creature came to her full bosom—the slightest pale swell of which was visible in the cleavage of her clean blouse—it shuddered with delight and then crept in.

With a rusty squeal a door opened somewhere. The strange old man in the wide-brimmed hat and tattered cloak who walked over to Wu-Lin without making a sound was none other than Professor Krolock. Gazing long and hard at the young woman with her knees on the floor and both arms dangling from the chains in some horrible parody of a cheer, the old man said, "Simply awful." But his voice didn't hold an ounce of emotion. "When I heard those curs boasting about how good the girl they'd caught looked, I thought it might be you and had to come see. Sure enough, I was right. Bit by a 'chatterbug,' were you? But I'll be—you still draw breath! I suppose I should put you at peace."

The old man's right hand vanished into his cloak, and when it appeared again, it clutched a quill pen. It was an ordinary pen, but the tip was razor sharp. The quill was from a supernatural creature called a messiah bird. That fowl sang only once in a decade, and only three times total in its lifetime—and those that heard its song were guaranteed to meet with misfortune.

Perhaps the girl sensed the professor's presence, because Wu-Lin's limp body once again showed signs of life. Her face rose. "Help . . . me . . . ," she said.

At the same time, what looked like a black spring came out of her cleavage and made a powerful bound for the professor's throat. The quill pen jabbed right through it.

Skewered in midair, the bug continued to struggle for a while, but then quickly settled down. Shaking it off so that it fell at his feet, the professor wasted no time in crushing it, and then placed his left hand on Wu-Lin's neck. Due perhaps to the insect's poison, the girl's face was so horribly swollen her own parents wouldn't have recognized her immediately. Quickly donning a puzzled expression, the professor remarked, "How unusual. Such tenacity. Speak, child. I shall hang on your every word."

"Tell my sister . . . about this . . . Get the bead back . . . for her . . ."

"Understood," the professor said with a grave nod. Behind his paternal demeanor dwelt a fearful shadow. "I shall get it back. Count on that. It shouldn't prove terribly difficult," he snickered.

Wu-Lin's expression rapidly drained away. Swollen to twice their normal size, her lips framed one final and almost inaudible remark.

Gently shutting the girl's eyelids after her head lolled to the side, the professor intoned what sounded like a spell, and then turned his back on her. Shocked, he froze in his tracks. The old man gazed absentmindedly at the tall form that stood before him. It wasn't the bloody blade in the figure's right hand that kept the professor riveted, but rather his positively dazzling beauty.

"You! How long have you been there?!" the professor asked, a ring of admiration in his voice. "I can't believe you could be there without me noticing you. Never mind the fact that there were supposed to be lookouts posted up top. And tough ones, at that—strong enough to tear apart winged dragons with their bare hands."

The old man's gaze went to the ceiling, then instantly dropped again to the young man's sword.

"Oh, I see—they were no match for you after all, were they? What brings you here, then? Are you somehow connected to this girl? I'll have you know, I was only here to see to her in her last moments. I never harmed a hair on her head!"

Not speaking a word, the shadowy figure made his way to Wu-Lin's corpse. Stopping, he extended his left hand and pushed back the hair that'd fallen across the girl's brow. Perhaps that was the young man's way of honoring her.

It was D. The Hunter extended his still-closed left hand, and when he opened it before Wu-Lin's face and the professor spied the bead resting in his palm, the old man coughed loudly. As the professor effortlessly reached for the prize, D's five fingers closed.

"Pardon me. You may not have heard her, but the girl asked me to do something for her. She said to find the bead for her. That's no lie."

"Where's the girl's sister?" D inquired softly. Apparently he had caught a few of the girl's final words.

Coughing, the professor replied, "As I just finished saying, I'll gladly bring it to her." The old man spoke with perfect composure, extending his hand as he did so.

D's hand opened first. But there was no bead in it.

"Where have you hidden it, you scoundrel?!" the professor cried out in amazement. And then, in a strangely calm tone he added, "I see. Regardless of how you might've come to know about this girl, I applaud your sincerity in bringing back the bead. It would seem that the person she asked me to get it back from wasn't you. However, the bead couldn't possibly be of any significance to you. Why don't you simply name your price, and I'll purchase it. Then I can deliver it to her sister. Once there, I'll receive my remuneration, and everything will be wrapped up tidily. What say you?"

"Where's the girl's sister?" D repeated.

"Why, you wretched—"

"When you checked the girl for vital signs, she was already dead. Yet she managed to convey her wishes. And you weren't the only one to hear them."

"Oh. In other words, you hypothesize she'd have no problem with you delivering the bead, then?"

Slowly, D turned. The air froze.

The professor tried to back away but couldn't. It was the ghastly aura emanating from this young man alone that chilled him to the very bone.

"I . . . I don't know. Surely you could see that," the professor replied. He couldn't help but answer. "The girl didn't say at all."

"You knew the girl," D said, his sword rising smoothly. "This is the last time I'll ask you this. Where was she from?"

"Do you intend to . . . cut me down?" the professor asked. His gaze seemed to be hopelessly drawn to the tip of the blade poised right between his eyes. "Would you cut me down . . . me, an innocent man?"

A drop of fresh blood rolled slowly down the old man's forehead.

"Florence," the professor said in a hoarse voice. Shortly after that, as he thudded to his knees on the floor, he heard the sound of a door closing up above.

The professor was not quick to rise, but rather produced a handkerchief from inside his cloak and mopped the sweat from his brow. But no matter how he wiped at it, the sweat just kept pouring from him.

"I fear I must revise my earlier statement," the old man said, his words hugging the ground. "'It shouldn't prove terribly difficult . . .' That's a fine joke now. However, now that I've seen his face . . ."

The professor held a piece of rolled-up vellum. Spreading the thin animal hide on the floor with trembling hands, he knelt on the edges to hold it down while his right hand went into action. His fingers clasped the quill pen. Soon enough his right hand ceased trembling and he ran the pen over the vellum—the very pen that dripped with his own blood. While the eerie deed itself was similar to what'd he'd done to Wu-Lin on that early morn, the strokes of his pen were so much swifter now that the two cases couldn't be compared.

Just how much time drifted by in that basement where the shadow of death hung, no one could say.

"Finished," the professor declared. "I wouldn't call it perfect— though it should prove moderately useful."

Satisfaction and fatigue now sharing space on his countenance, the old man looked at the thin hide spread before him bearing D's features etched in minute detail.

II

Exiting a basement in the shopping district, Gilligan quickly headed for home. Just as he'd expected, the girl had told him everything she knew before dying an agonizing death. Her pained, fever-induced throes had left him satisfied, and he was of a mind to head off to one of the whorehouses he operated, but there was something he had to take care of before he did so.

Entering the gorgeous estate that stood at the southern tip of town, he didn't go to the main house, but rather to a fairly large outbuilding constructed to one side of the acre-and-a-half garden. As he did so, a number of dark, beastly forms moved toward him through the trees, but upon recognizing him as their master they soon disappeared again. Skillfully making his way across the stepping stones, he arrived at a wooden door studded with hobnails and pressed against it lightly. As it creaked open, Gilligan disappointedly clucked, "Some folks can't do anything right." But he seemed to reconsider that remark as he grinned broadly and headed inside.

A sweet scent tickled his nose almost instantly. The fragrance was a blend of perfume and aphrodisiacs. It was such a heavy aroma that one whiff would be enough to make any ordinary person's head reel.

Beyond the door lay a vast hall, and in the far wall there were a number of doors. Not approaching any of them, Gilligan spoke instead from the very center of the hall. His voice, which wasn't particularly loud or intimidating, sounded almost mechanical. Perhaps it was meant to let everyone know the information he was about to divulge was of grave import. "It's me—Gilligan. Are you there, Egbert? Gyohki? Samon? Shin? Twin?"

After a short pause, replies came from the various doors.

"You bet."

"Yes."

"I'm here, all right."

"Sure."

"Urrrrr . . ."

The first voice was heavy, the second was a woman's, the third had a youthful vigor to it, and the one that followed it was hoarse. However, it was by no means certain that the order in which they'd replied matched that in which they'd been called. Each voice sounded as if it came from all of the doors, while conversely each had a mysterious ring to it that made the listener wonder if they'd heard it correctly. Particularly strange was the last of the replies. It was unmistakably the snarl of a beast.

As if he hadn't even noticed, Gilligan said, "A terrible situation has developed," as he turned his face alone to each of the doors. "A little lady came to an antique shop that's under my purview, and she had a certain bead doodad that she wished to have appraised. The item in question was absolutely unbelievable. Why, even the antique dealer himself didn't know what he was really dealing with. But he's quite a bookworm. As luck would have it, he'd looked through some incredibly old documents that helped him out. There was only a single line about it in there, and this is what it said—"

Taking a breath, Gilligan told them what it was.

No one spoke behind the closed doors, but the shock waves certainly echoed back.

"Now, this doesn't mean anything to you," Gilligan said, his words charged with a certain vehemence. "But it'll prove useful to me. More than you could ever imagine."

Somewhere, one of them laughed. Mockingly. "Sure enough. That'd suit your tastes to a tee. But do me a favor and make sure I never have to see that look on your face again. It makes my stomach turn."

"So, what are you suggesting we do?" another voice asked. The voice was that of the woman, and was so seductive it could make people quiver.

"The little lady came by the bead in the village of Florence, and you're going to go up there and find me a new bead because some dirty thief stole the other bead from me. At the moment, I've sent someone to catch him as quickly as possible. But to be perfectly frank, I have my doubts about whether they'll get it back."

It seemed that the human slug named Gilligan actually had an excellent grasp of the situation. For just a short time earlier, a quiet but deadly three-sided conflict had played out in the streets of the entertainment district.

"Oh," the hoarse voice said, his interjection carrying a lengthy tail. "So, the thief is a power to be dealt with, then?"

"One of my bodyguards just happened to know him. Apparently he has some strange trick he can do. He's pretty famous in the northwest corner of the Frontier—a man by the name of Toto."

"I see," the youthful voice said with admiration. "I've heard of him, too. He's got a nickname, right? 'Backwards Toto,' if I recall. Apparently there's never been anything he went after that he didn't end up getting."

"One more thing—the reason I've gone to all the trouble of getting famed Frontier enforcers like yourselves instead of using my own people is because the Nobility are obviously involved in this. I assume you're all familiar with the history of Florence."

"You mean the Florence Nobility?" the hoarse voice muttered. "Hell, that was a good thousand years ago."

Gilligan nodded. There was the sound of meshing gears from the loop of steel that restrained his jaw. "Precisely. Life there isn't much different now from in any other northern fishing town. But from what the girl told me, the village elders seem to be in an uproar, and there's talk about Nobles coming out of the sea again this summer."

"Nobles that come from the sea?" the woman said, her voice like the tinkling of a bell. "That's patently absurd," she laughed. "We don't yet know the Nobility's greatest weaknesses. However, any child could tell you water poses a serious threat to them."

"We can't necessarily say that applies to every last one of them, you know," said the owner of the grave voice. "If you'll consider the history of the area for a moment, you'll see what I mean. There are bizarre legends connected to the place. Perhaps the tales that have been handed down during the past millennia have finally come true."

"The little lady didn't even know what the bead was worth. Why, she just took something lying around the house and came here to get a little money for it, never understanding what it really was. How unfortunate for her," Gilligan chortled. "It would seem her grandfather back home might've known something, but apparently he never told the rest of the family about it. Perhaps the quickest way to find out where the bead came from or how to get another one would be to ask him."

"Fine. After all, locking horns with the Nobility sounds like fun. But what kind of compensation are we talking about for the danger we'll be facing? We're not all into the same twisted shit you are, you know."

To the youthful voice's query, Gilligan calmly replied, "I'll turn over all of my land and my entire fortune to whoever brings me back that bead. As you can see, I had the paperwork drawn up on my way back here. Whosoever brings back the bead should go see the lawyer named Fearing and he'll do the rest for you."

"What happens if two of us bring it back?" the feminine voice asked. Her tone was forebodingly deep.

"If there're two of you, each gets half. Three, and you split it three ways," Gilligan said, seeming to egg his guests on.

Not only did the zeal in the voices of the other five rise a notch in response, but they also took on a cruel and calculating ring.

"Who else knows about the bead?" a dignified voice inquired.

"Just the girl's older sister—a woman by the name of Su-In. There were two others, but one of them got taken out while he was chasing after the thing, and the other would seem to be a guest of mine, oddly enough. Come to mention it, he should be at 'The Ox' now."

"The Ox" was the name of a bar Gilligan owned.

"Will he be getting involved in this matter?"

"I can't rightly say. I suppose that'll be up to him. An old friend of mine introduced me to him, but he's not exactly like normal folks. It's Professor Krolock."

Every sound died out.

"'Backwards Toto' and 'Professor Krolock'? Man, that's even more fun than the Nobility!" the youthful voice exclaimed in a tone laden with excitement and tension.

Several seconds passed.

"Actually, there's someone else, too," Gilligan said in a solemn tone as a troubled look swept over his barely human countenance.

"So there's another person after the bead. Why not come right out and say who it is? Are you afraid you'll scare us or something?"

"Pretty much," Gilligan said with a nod. His whole body stiffened, and with a mechanical clanking he backed away a few steps—he'd just been subjected to emanations of powerful hatred.

When you became a person of some stature in a community, you had to play host to famous warriors, bodyguards, and Hunters and see to it they weren't left wanting where drinking, gambling, and whoring were concerned. The skill level of the enforcers said person could gather when he found himself in a jam not only reflected on his status, but could also mean the difference between life and death. However, the more renowned his visitors were for their abilities, the more intense their dispositions tended to be. Relying on such characters was like clinging to a ticking time bomb.

The palpable sense of hatred rapidly faded. Chilling laughter then flowed from all of the doors.

"My, you certainly had us going," the female voice tittered.

"You surely did. C'mon, Mr. Gilligan. Stop playing games and tell us who it is already."

"Very well," Gilligan said, his whole body seeming to quiver with joy. "The Vampire Hunter D."

At that moment, he could sense nothing from any of the others. It was as if they'd all been struck dead.

After a brief pause, Gilligan added, "Does that sound interesting or what?" His voice trembled as he put the question to them.

"Intriguing," said the fifth voice. But that was the door where only beastly growls had been heard earlier. Perhaps whoever was behind the door controlled demonic creatures.

"Now, that's what I like to hear," Gilligan said, his tone returning to normal. "Rest assured, he only helped out the girl. As for the bead, he doesn't even know it exists. What's more, he's a heartless type who doesn't undertake anything unless he's been employed, and even then he only works to dispose of the Nobility. There's not a chance in a million of him sticking his nose into this, I tell you. So relax. You'll set out tomorrow. I'll arrange to cover your traveling expenses tonight, too."

"Do it now," the youthful voice said. "You think any of us are gonna hang around until tomorrow? No one here's thinking about anything except how to beat the rest to the punch. I'm leaving right away."

"So am I."

"Me, too," said another man.

"As am I," the female voice added.

"I'm going, too."

Gilligan's features twisted, and his face collapsed into a grin. If there was ever a smile the world didn't want to see, it was his.

"You're all I thought you'd be. Here's your money," Gilligan said, taking some golden cards from one of his pockets and dropping them on the floor. "In the Northern Frontier, you can use these cards at any store. Or if the conditions are less than optimal, you can turn them in for money at a bank somewhere. I'm counting on you."

And saying that, Gilligan turned his back to them. The instant he closed the front door to the building he sensed movements behind him, but he headed toward the main house without saying a word.

The stillness of the wee hours had descended upon the lavish estate. The household staff was asleep. With a grating sound echoing behind him, Gilligan advanced to the end of the hall and climbed the staircase. His bedroom was on the second floor, thus he went up a second flight of stairs. None of his staff or his henchmen had permission to go up there. The top of the staircase was blocked by a steel door. Taking out a key, he unlocked it.

Once inside, he switched on the lights and looked around at the room that surrounded him. Somehow, it was reminiscent of a factory. There was so much engineering equipment and material like plastic and steel that there wasn't even room to walk around. And in the center of that mess rested a black lump. As Gilligan gazed at it, his eyes seemed to fill with a deep emotion.

"Ah, at last," the human slug said in a feverish tone. "Finally, my dreams will be realized. Then I can bid farewell to this squalid business and the lowly human company. And leave with you."

There was a table off to one side that had a bottle of liquor and some glasses. As Gilligan poured himself one drink after another, his eyes drifted back and forth between the black object and the ceiling. The room's ceiling was dome-shaped. A single line curved all the way across the center of it.

After completely emptying the bottle, Gilligan left his "factory." Going down the first flight of stairs, he was about to keep walking, but instead stopped right where he was. A black shadow stood at the end of the corridor.

The thought that it might be a burglar popped into Gilligan's head, but the heavy man quickly froze with astonishment.

The reason the intruder had looked like a shadow was because of his black raiment. And the face above that dark clothing was resplendent in its beauty.

"You . . ." he mumbled, forgetting what he wanted to ask. "You're D, I take it?"

"And you're the one who had the bug bite that girl Wu-Lin?" His voice, like his face, was gorgeous.

And yet Gilligan couldn't so much as lift a finger. Out of fear. Only his tongue could move.

"How did you know . . . to look here? And right after I left the girl . . . And I had watchdogs in the garden . . ." the slug-like man babbled, blinking his eyes. He was trying to get the cold sweat out of them.

A second later, D was right in front of him. Gilligan didn't even know when the Hunter'd had time to move. It was almost as if the stillness of night was loath to trouble the gorgeous young man about minor matters such as distance.

"Don't tell me . . . You know, don't you . . . about the bead?" Of course, he was basically admitting that he'd used poison to draw the information out of Wu-Lin.

A flash of silver mowed right across the fat man's chin. Sparks shot out.

D pulled his sword away.

"Too bad," Gilligan said, stroking the bar by the base of his neck. "This baby is made of Zeramium steel. Had it custom built way

back in the Capital. Shoot, it'd take a laser an hour to cut into it a fraction of an inch."

The wind brushed by his neck. There was a loud clang at his feet. It was the sound of the bar that'd shielded his chin falling to the floor.

Gilligan felt his hair was rising on end.

"Don't think that it stopped me," D said softly. "When someone gets bitten by a 'chatterbug,' they go through more than thirty minutes of agony before they die."

Once again the Hunter's sword made a horizontal slash, and Gilligan followed it intently until it returned to its sheath. His field of view then shook. Head reeling wildly and crimson splashing into his eyes, he saw the figure in the black coat leaving again.

Gilligan was rooted where he stood until the young man went down the staircase and disappeared. All the while, his head and torso were only connected by a single flap of skin—and blood was pumping from the wound like water from a fountain. Both arms clicked as they moved. Taking hold of the head as it drooped against the right side of his body, his arms lifted it clumsily. Even after the two pieces were lined up, bright blood continued to gush from the slice that remained between them.

"Damn it . . . that hurts . . . ," the head said. But it was turned toward the back. "Damn . . . That's not right . . . Ow . . . Shit, that hurts . . ."

His hands rotated his head a hundred and eighty degrees. This time it was a little left of being on center.

"Well . . . Good enough, I guess . . . Ow . . . But it'll take more than this . . . to kill me."

As he said that, his lips turned violet and his face went pale as paraffin.

Now in a state that would've long since killed an ordinary human, Gilligan slowly changed direction and once again began climbing the stairs. Surely it was the work of the machinery amplifying his dying strength, but the fact that he even managed to open the door and get into the room bordered on miraculous.

"Almost there . . . Just a little more . . . Shit . . . I'll be damned if I'll die here after coming this far . . . Damn, it hurts . . . Hurts like hell . . . I don't ever want it to hurt like this again . . . Shit . . . D, you bastard . . . Just you wait . . ."

And then, with his head held securely the whole time, the town's kingpin rattled mechanically toward a black object, strange cries of pain ringing from him all the way.

Several minutes later there was the unpleasant sputter of a motor, and the line across the ceiling began to grow thicker. The black line let in the pale glow of dawn, and before long the purple clouds of daybreak, and the whole heavens where they billowed lay revealed.

To the North Sea

CHAPTER 3

I

There was nothing save a single lamp to light the wooden shack. Windows rimmed with the remains of shattered glass let the icy wind blow in mercilessly, sharp as a sword and cold as the breath of the frost demons that inhabited the northern sea. The dozen or more people seated inside on the wooden benches were left shivering. One side of the shack was wide open, and across from it lay sea and sky as dull and gray as lead. Coming across a limitless expanse of cold water, the wind was naturally freezing, and the old-fashioned oil heater set in the middle of the shack served little purpose. Impressive as its size was, its performance was pitiful.

If you approached the entrance and looked far off into the distance—about seven miles across from the shack—the silhouette of land loomed blackly like the back of some behemoth. Hook-beaked sea birds swooped down, trying to smash through the crests of the mighty breakers. In order to pierce the armored exterior of the shellfish they relished, the birds were able to increase the molecular density of their beaks and teeth, but for that short time their mass also increased. Because of this, any birds that didn't manage to burst through the waves at high speed and crack open the shellfish would soon find themselves unable to pull out of their dive.

The shadowy form on the opposite shore stretched on forever to either side, and the water between them seemed like an ocean between two islands, but it was actually a canal, and the two pieces of land were siblings that came together again several hundred miles away. Both those who wished to cross over to the opposite side of this vast channel and those headed much further inland came to this little harbor and boarded the regularly scheduled ferry. It was a large ship that could accommodate two hundred passengers or more. For people seeking to avoid the decrepit overland routes and the various supernatural beasts and creatures that prowled them, this one modern convenience proved indispensable. Its only drawback was that weather and waves could stop service indefinitely, causing delays of days or weeks while they waited for the weather to clear again. But usually the captain's skill and guts were enough to get them through. The ferry made the round trip six times a day.

The ship the people now awaited was the first of the afternoon and the third of the day. More than a dozen passengers were waiting, and true to Frontier tradition, most of them were farmers or merchants. The exceptions were a group of women who looked like part of the "gay trade," a priest, and several men with swords and spears who were apparently roving warriors.

Particularly conspicuous in this group was a tall young man leaning back against one wall. He seemed to be carefully contemplating something, and his alarmingly good looks as he held that pensive pose caught the eyes of the rest of the passengers. And yet, the women there, who were well-skilled at getting close to men, didn't do anything. Not only could they not approach him, but they couldn't even speak to him. The scent of danger that radiated along with his beauty seemed to set off some instinctive sense humans had about matters of life and death. As if intentionally disregarding him, a farming couple with a child threw themselves into small talk with a traveling merchant, the warriors had a few drinks together, and the hut in general was filled with a fair bit of hubbub.

Suddenly catching sight of a dark shape, the ticket vendor at the dock across from the shack shouted, "Here she comes!"

Inside the shack, where the air had been so cold it'd seemed more like winter than just before summer, the mood lightened instantly.

"Right on schedule."

"Looks like I'll make it in time."

"Where you headed?"

"The village of Lugosi—got some medicine to sell there, you know."

A small blob of color wove through all of the chattering passengers. It was a young child, the son of the farming couple. Five or six years of age, his somewhat plump form quickly cut across the hut, discarded the candy wrapper he had in his hand in a trash barrel by the door, and then dashed right back again.

But just then, a powerful voice as loud as thunder roared, "What the hell do you think you're doing?!" and the little boy sprawled across the floor.

Simultaneously, the eyes of the startled folks turned and focused on the three brutes who had risen angrily from the bench by the door. Everyone knew that this couldn't be good. Armed with swords and spears, the men looked to be warriors. Though that trade generally consisted of wandering the Frontier and lending their skills to the war on monstrous creatures for a price, it attracted more than its share of uncouth characters. Well aware that the slightest problem might be a chance for them to cash in on their expertise, such people had no qualms about stirring up trouble themselves or threatening and blackmailing others when low on funds.

"Little bastard! You kicked my damn sword!" shouted a glowering individual who was by far the hairiest of the trio. Because he also happened to have a wool coat on, he actually looked more like a demonic beast than someone who might dispose of such creatures.

The other two warriors were quick to add their indignation.

"He's got no manners at all!"

"Where the hell are his parents at?!"

One was a bald man clad in battered armor. The other wore slacks and a flimsy shirt that left his overdeveloped musculature quite evident. A single glance was enough to confirm them both as the worst kind of thugs that could ever be found.

"Darn it, Calvin!" the boy's mother cried out in a tight voice as she ran to him, while the boy's father walked over to the men.

"Please accept our apologies," the farmer said. "He is just a child, after all."

"I ain't accepting shit!" the furry warrior growled as he slapped the hilt of his sword with one hand. "This here's the tool of my trade. You know, even the least little nick to it might cost me my life someday. Then what would you have to say? You trying to tell me my life don't mean a damn thing to you or something?"

"Don't be ridiculous," the boy's father replied, already deathly pale.

The rest of the crowd glared at the warrior reproachfully, but when his cohorts looked around, the others all turned their eyes to the floor.

"Here—I hope this will set things right again." Pulling a cloth pouch from his pocket, the boy's father forced a few coins into the man's hand.

Glancing at the money, the man bellowed, "You gotta be kidding me!" and swung his hairy arm through the air. The coins clattered noisily across the stone floor, and the air seemed to freeze solid. "If there's one thing I can't stand, it's someone who thinks that money solves everything. I'm gonna teach you and your brat some manners!"

The warrior's hairy paw caught the father by the front of his shirt. The father tried to say something, but couldn't.

Suddenly, there was a swift movement through the otherwise frozen world. The boy had just tugged at the waist of a handsome young man who was leaning back against the wall. "Mister—help me!" the child sobbed, perhaps sensing with youthful intuition that this young man would be up to the task.

But the young man didn't move. He didn't so much as look at the boy.

On the other hand, the three warriors *did* react.

"You gonna do something about this?" asked the man wearing the armor plate. His tone was a good deal more threatening than that of his hairy companion. He was probably the leader of the trio. "Make no mistake; we ain't having a beauty contest here. You'd do well to keep your trap shut."

"Good advice," was all the young man said. He didn't look at the trio. But it wasn't because he was afraid to meet their eyes—and everyone there could tell as much. "This doesn't concern me. Neither this child's request nor your threats have any bearing on me. However—" the youth said, slowly turning his gorgeous and pale visage toward the other men, "never address me again."

His words were soft. They didn't carry the tone of a command. He was merely conveying his wishes.

The men grew stiff. The hairy one's cheek started to twitch, and the man in armor swallowed hard.

While it wasn't clear whether or not he'd seen the results of his glare and his brief remarks, the young man turned back the way he'd been facing.

Suddenly, the bald warrior raised his right hand—in it, he held a long spear. Throwing it at this range, he couldn't miss. If anyone had noticed it, it was hurled with such speed there was nothing they could do about it.

But then the spear stopped in midair. With a firm crack like a rawhide whip had wrapped around it, the weapon was caught right near the middle of the shaft by a pale hand that shot out from the left side.

The bald man's eyes bulged in their sockets.

The hand was that of a woman. Easily adjusting her grip on the weapon she'd seized with unbelievable skill, then rising with determination, the woman had a large frame that ran a tad to the heavy side. She had to be around twenty years old. With an average face that wouldn't have made her stand out in a crowd, she'd actually stood right next to the merchant group without any of those talkative fellows ever noticing her, and the three toughs were frankly surprised to find she'd been sitting there. However, as she held the lengthy spear in one hand and glared at the three of them, her eyes and her expression were infused with a solemn air that made it clear she wouldn't let this outrageous action stand. Needless to say, this determination came with the kind of skill it took to pluck a whizzing spear out of the air.

"Stop it. This is no way for a grown man to behave. Why don't you think for a moment about where we are? Just what would you do if this spear had hit someone else, huh?!" the woman said, both her words and bearing unbelievably brisk and spirited as they overwhelmed the trio of warriors.

Finally, the hairy one snorted, "You bitch . . ." His eyes had a dangerous look in them.

Now free of the hairy fist, the boy's father hastened back to his wife and child.

"Oh, so now you're gonna pick on a girl, are you?" the woman said in a gentle tone as she coolly returned the glares the vicious eyes had trained on her.

The hairy warrior's left hand buzzed into action—he'd just undone the latch on his long sword. Now there was nothing left to do but draw.

"Please, stop it already," someone said. It was a priest in an old brick-red cassock. But in this case "priest" didn't mean the leader of the sort of strange new religions popping up like mad in the Capital and its surrounding areas. The kind of holy men that traveled the harsh Frontier were apostles of primitive faiths that held the very foundations of humanity's vital energies. Due to the fact that he was bound to have some incredible skills or spells at his disposal, this was the man of whom the trio of thugs had been wariest. On closer inspection, the old priest's graying hair was thinning, and his eyes and skin both lacked vitality. Thinking that the holy man would soon back down if threatened, the warriors had gone into action, but when the priest stood up, he actually proved a disturbing sight.

"What the hell do you want?! Keep out of this!" the bald warrior shouted back at the holy man.

"Stop it. If you're set on continuing this, you should have no problem doing so once we've all reached our destination. If blood's to be spilled, spilling it now with this journey ahead will only lead to remorse. You should at least hold off until we get to where we want to go," the old priest added.

His words found some support.

"That's right. You don't choose a place like this to go stirring up trouble."

"Men your size should try acting their age. Buffoons!"

The trio glared at the bar girls, and the women turned away disdainfully.

Things had gone so far that the warriors couldn't just drop the matter, and yet they couldn't very well cut down everyone who stood against them, either. The thugs exchanged bloodshot glances.

The reprieve everyone had been waiting for came in the form of the ticket seller's voice as he cried out, "Okay, get in line. Line it up now. The ship's here."

"Say, mister—you were pretty great," said a bar girl who approached from the forward seats, her words causing the young man to look up ever so slightly.

They were toward the back of the ship. Under the black vinyl canopy there were ten rows of benches on either side, with each seating four passengers. Beyond the little window of semi-translucent plastic, the dull gray sea was baring its foamy teeth. It was fairly rough.

Less than ten minutes had passed since the ferry had left the dock. Its speed was twelve knots, or almost fifteen miles per hour. Originally procured from the Capital, the ship's gasoline-powered engine was huge but rather antiquated.

"Those three talked tough, but one look from you had them shaking in their boots. Not bad for someone as young as you. You must've come through a few tight jams with that sword of yours," the woman said, turning her feverish gaze to the lavishly decorated blade cradled in his powerful arms. "Still, you'd do well to watch yourself. I'm sure they haven't forgotten about you. And I don't suppose you'll be safe even in here. But I sure wouldn't step outside if I were you," the woman said, her tone growing heated. "So, what's your name anyhow? If we're headed the same way once we reach shore, I was thinking maybe . . ."

The bar girl's hand gently brushed against that of the young man.

"There is one thing you can do for me."

This sudden remark from him caught the woman off-guard. "Um, sure," she stammered, nodding reflexively.

"You told me I shouldn't go outside, but there's someone on the stern that interests me—the man who jumped on just as the ferry was pulling away. Would you be so kind as to see what sort of fellow he is?"

Squinting at him, the woman asked, "Is someone after you?"

A glimmer of gold disappeared into the cleavage of her blouse.

"Will that suffice? I'd appreciate it."

Fishing the coin out with great haste and staring at it in amazement, the bar girl then gave a nod of obvious delight and headed off to the stern of the ship.

At just that moment, cries of fright rang out from the front of the seating section. It sounded like the boy and his parents. The cries of the child resounded particularly loudly, and the father's shout of "What are you doing?" soon became a shriek of pain.

The heavy footsteps that closed on the young man were those of two of the warriors.

"Care to come with us for a little bit?" the hairy thug said, tossing his jaw toward the ferry's stern.

Looking up at the man in armor right beside him, the young man asked, "Where's the third guy?"

"Sheesh. That's the least of your concerns, bub," the man in the armor spat.

The child seemed utterly terrified as he stared up at his pair of captors with a vacant gaze.

"If you're worried about this brat, you'll give us some of your time. Step outside and just see for yourself."

II

As she sensed someone drawing closer, the woman spun around reflexively. Even after she saw that it was the bald warrior, no fear or surprise crept into her expression. "What do you want?" she asked. Her tone was the epitome of calm.

"You caused me a hell of a lot of embarrassment," the bald man growled, the head of his spear gleaming just before his face. It was the only light on this gloomy day. Aside from the lead-gray sky and sea and the white wake of the ferry, there was only a mass of black cloud that seemed to follow the ship at the mercy of the wind.

"That's funny," the woman said, a smile surfacing on her lips. "The end of your spear is shining. As bad as the weather is, I guess there's a ray of light out there somewhere. The sun is shining. You know, where I come from, the winter's long and summer's over before you know it," the woman continued somewhat nostalgically, and the second she finished, a flash of white light shot at her chest.

As the woman sprang to the right with a speed that was staggering given her general build, the head of the spear twirled around after her, leaving a glittering trail. But the spearhead met only thin air.

The bald warrior's eyes were wide with surprise, but it was still remarkable that he only halted for a heartbeat before stabbing straight ahead again with his spear.

There was a brisk slap.

"What the hell?!" the man gasped, this time driven to comment by his astonishment.

The head of his spear had stopped an inch shy of the woman's ample bosom, caught in her hands. It was sandwiched between her joined palms.

"Ouf!" the man grunted as his muscles bulged. Shoulders and chest, arms and legs—they all seemed swollen to nearly twice their normal size. But the tip of the spear didn't budge. It wouldn't tremble in the slightest, as if it were lodged into one of the iron trees of Lamarck.

"You like that?" the woman said, her smile looking a bit pained. "Not the greatest trick in the world, but it'd be more than enough to snap the head off this. Isn't this one of the precious tools of your trade?"

The bald man didn't answer. His face swelled in a heartbeat, and vermilion flooded into his cheeks. It was almost as if all of the blood in his body had rushed into his head. The man then let out a long grunt.

A shaken look on her face, the woman started to rise steadily.

Incredibly enough, the man lifted his seven-foot-long spear high over his head with a grown woman still clinging to the end of it.

"Don't let go if you don't want to," the bald warrior told her. "Go ahead and break the end off. I'm just gonna dunk you in the water anyway. The cold'll be enough to stop your heart for sure. Feel like letting go? You do that and I'll impale you in midair!"

And then, after a cruel reprieve of a few seconds, the man prepared to spin his spear around.

At that very moment, the woman he held up in the air sprang higher. The spear was still for a moment as the warrior tried to compensate for the sudden loss of the woman's weight, and in that brief moment her pale hand chopped at the weapon's shaft. Watching out of the corner of her eye as the spear tip flipped end-over-end to knife gently into the water, the woman landed spectacularly on the cramped deck. Exhaling lightly, she stuck both hands out in front of her body. Her left leg was bent somewhat to support her weight, while her right foot was one step forward and balanced on its toes, like a cat. Given this woman's skill, she could probably do whatever she wanted to with that right leg now that it didn't have to hold her up.

"Not too shabby," the bald man said as he delivered a loud slap to his own face. "You surprise me. But if I can't spear you, how 'bout I just use the pole?"

Something whipped through the air. It sounded like a whistle.

To evade that thrust of ungodly speed, the woman twisted her body and leapt back.

"Take that! And that! And that!" the man shouted with thrust after thrust, never letting the woman get very far away.

After a second leap and a third, the woman reached the stern. A horse snorted. Not all of the travelers had been on foot. Though she tried to circle around them, she couldn't—the rounded end of the weapon had a force far beyond the earlier strikes when it stopped about a foot and a half shy of the woman's face. Almost as if pierced by the tenacity and bloodlust pouring from her opponent, the woman's face was soon covered with beads of sweat.

"Looks like we both mean business," the bald warrior said, revealing his yellowed teeth. Just then, his eyes slipped a bit off of her and focused on something else—a gorgeous figure who had just appeared next to the woman from the rear door to the ship's cabin. "What the hell do you want?!" the man growled in a low voice.

The slight alterations to his tone and the glint in his eyes made the woman turn to look, too.

"You're—" she mumbled.

"You gonna try and stop me?" the bald man asked, having somewhat rekindled his murderous intent.

There was no reply. But in lieu of one, a strangely indescribable miasma spread around them like thick honey, making the man back away instinctively. Dripping with the same cold sweat as the woman, the thug found his eyes filled by the sight of the young man, and his graceful good looks seemed to drive the warrior's thoughts toward a philosophical abyss.

†

"Well, well. Are we gonna do this?" the armored warrior said, his right hand reaching for the grip of his sword.

"Lemme go!" the boy cried.

The furry warrior looked down at the kid scornfully, and then shifted his eyes to the young man before him. "Aren't you gonna do anything, pretty boy? You're a lot colder than I thought."

The young man didn't answer him. Even as his field of view was occupied by the innocent face of the boy wriggling against those hairy arms, neither his eyes nor his gorgeous face betrayed the slightest glimmer of human emotion.

Behind the young man were the boy's mother and father.

"Please, you've got to do something!" said one.

"Save him! I beg of you!" the other shouted.

Both parents sounded like they were on the brink of tears. But another voice came on top of their pleas. "I specifically told you not to pick a fight with me."

"Oh, the stud speaks at last!"

"When you get to the next world, be sure to tell the gatekeeper exactly how I killed you," said the other warrior.

With a whine from their scabbards, both thugs drew their blades.

"The kid is in the way," the young man said casually.

The hirsute warrior shook his head. "No, he ain't in the way at all. At least, not for *me*."

"Stop it!" the mother shouted, her shrill cry shaking the chilly air.

"Have it your way then," the young man said, his right hand reaching for his own longsword. While his opponents were thugs, it was also clear they must've lived through countless battles. The fact that he was willing to not only make enemies of the two of them but also to let them draw first had to be due to more than mere self-confidence. "You don't have to let him go if you don't want to. But don't let my blade get away from you, either."

What the young man had stated was really quite obvious. No one could defend himself from an enemy's blade without seeing it, and the pair of thugs weren't taking their eyes off the end of his sword.

His longsword came down with a *swoosh!* The movement looked gentle enough, but slashed fiercely through the air. Just as it was about to reach the planks of the deck, the blade stopped. The two warriors stood staring at it.

There was a whistle. Following the very same path, the young man's blade began to rise. And then—

Watching, the thugs raised their swords again, too. They raised them high. As if following the lead of the young man, who was poised with his blade high over his head, they both took the very same stance. The gesture was in perfect synchronization. The only difference was they didn't take the same step forward that the young man had.

The young man's sword dropped coolly. The blades that the two thugs brought down at exactly the same time met nothing but thin air, and bright blood shot up from the head of the hairy warrior like a pillar of smoke. Without a sound, he dropped backward.

"Mommy!" the boy shouted, breaking free from the hairy arm and dashing away. The tiny figure bumped into the young man's leg.

A horizontal slash buzzed through the air toward the young man's cheek. It was the armored warrior's second attack. Oddly enough, his first blow had come from above—just like that of his furry compatriot.

Pale sparks flew off the blade harshly. The young man had parried the blow with his peerless skill.

"Shit!" the man in armor shouted as he pulled his blade back again, but he then made a strange move. Holding his blade at eye-level, he moved both hands to the right as quickly as he could and kicked off the ship's deck in a mighty bound. A second later, his chest was pierced cleanly by a thrust from the blade the young man held exactly the same way. Falling face-first without a sound, by the time the body finally thudded against the deck, the young man's blade was back in the scabbard at his waist.

As the young man's hand came away from his weapon's hilt, the boy shouted with joy, "You did it, mister! You did it!" His previous fears were now completely forgotten as he rushed over to the young man from behind. Blushing, the boy leapt for the young man's back.

A second later, two silvery flashes shot past each other.

The back of the young man he was about to cling to was no longer there, and after the boy flipped head over heels and hit the floor, his right arm was missing from the shoulder-down.

A bloody mist hung in the air.

Strangely enough, the boy immediately leapt up again. Pressing down on his shoulder as blood gushed from it, he was rapidly losing the color from his face, where not a fragment of his earlier innocence remained. Filled with the sly villainy of an old man, his eyes were trained on his own right arm, which had fallen at the young man's feet—an arm that held a sharp needle in its plump little hand.

"A poison needle, eh?" the young man muttered. "You may have thought you had me fooled, but I'm sorry to disappoint you. Still, it's a strange sort of talent you have—the parents and the bar girl aren't real people. Of course, these thugs aren't either. State your name!"

There was a sword dripping with blood stuck right under the boy's nose, but he only laughed in a low voice. It wasn't the voice of a child. Rather, it was the tone of a man untold centuries old and heavy with wrinkles. "How long have you known?" he asked.

"From the very beginning, when the farmer pulled out his money back at the landing. The coins were fine, but the bills mixed in with them were blank slips of paper. Next, there was the bar girl. At a distance she would've passed, but she got too close. You probably wanted her to get in good with me in case these two thugs screwed up, but you were sloppy. That was the first time I ever touched a woman's hand and couldn't feel a pulse," said the young man.

The boy—who was most likely a bizarre old man in flesh and spirit and every other regard aside from that youthful visage—listened without saying a word. But at this point, he leaned back and laughed out loud. "Oh, so that's what happened? Up against someone like you, I should've had every possible angle covered. I see my preparations were inadequate. But I should expect no less from the

Vampire Hunter D. Well, at least I did away with that impudent little wench while I was here."

"You're in for a disappointment there," a mirthful voice laughed from the stern.

The boy turned around.

The woman was standing there. Behind her well-rounded figure was the most gorgeous young man in black.

"You mean—you?!" the boy screamed, his words directed not at the woman, but rather at this new, beautiful figure.

"My name is Glen," the first young man said, as if nothing at all had transpired. "Over there's the man you're looking for. So damn handsome, I can't even begin to compare. What, would you prefer it was his blade that dispatched you to the next world?"

"Oh, so that's what happened. It's just been one screwup after another today," the boy said, laughing loudly once again. His face was pale, but nothing could extinguish the malevolent flames that burned in his eyes. "I figured there was no sense running myself ragged getting out here, so I came on my own. But then when I saw a guy at the harbor that was just far too good-looking, well, I jumped to the wrong conclusion. Well, if you've come this far, D, we must be headed to the same place."

Lips that made women and men alike swoon moved as D said, "You work for Gilligan?"

"I suppose I do, at that. I'm not surprised you've heard as much. 'Shin the Manipulator' is the name. Just so I don't give the rest of them an edge on me, I suppose I should tell you there're four others headed for the village. They're all enforcers hand-picked by Gilligan, and each and every one of them has some sort of weird ability. But interestingly enough, none of us knows what any of the others looks like. I'll give you their names, though. There's Egbert, Samon, the 'dawn demon' Gyohki, and Twin. And I can't tell you how much I'd appreciate it if you could knock some of them off before the next time we meet. Of course, they might just take your life first, which would also work for me."

The ship must've hit rough seas, because the deck then pitched to starboard—the side to Shin's back.

D raised his right hand to fend off a breaking wave.

Exhausted perhaps, the boy with the hoarse voice pulled away the hand that'd been pressed to his oozing wound and slumped against the deck. But as the little body then sailed into the air, the only things that could've kept Glen from catching him in flight when the young man slashed up from below with his blade were the desperation of the boy or the young man's own inattentiveness. The boy's body cleared the deck and was headed for the waves—but he never touched the surface of the water, instead sailing up along the side of the ship and into the air.

Upon spying the mass of black clouds floating high above them, the woman not surprisingly muttered, "That's impossible!"

Rapidly dwindling in the sky, the figure let his sneering words rain down to the trio on deck along with the gore from his wound. "This cloud is another of my puppets," he said with a laugh. "Never even saw the strings, did you? We'll meet again. And when we do, I'll see to it you pay for what you did to my arm."

"Not too shabby," Glen muttered, sheathing his blade. He didn't even glance at Shin, who'd dwindled to a mere speck.

The scattered bodies of thugs at his feet had changed into wooden dolls. Eight inches tall, the arms and legs attached to each were complete with joints. The roughly hewn faces and ragged clothes certainly bore some resemblance to the living men, with a sword made from a strip of wood. But what sort of sorcery had lent them their false life? Here was an almost incomprehensible foe.

"Wow—this one even has little veins filled with blood. That's some detailed craftsmanship. He's cut in exactly the same place that the live version was."

"So are these two . . ." the woman said with distaste as she looked down at her feet, where the boy's parents lay. They'd changed into dolls before her very eyes.

What Shin manipulated was puppets.

In the Capital and out on the Frontier, there were more than a few puppeteers who moved their creations with strings, magnets, or mechanical devices. Taking painted casings of tin or hollowed-out wood, they would construct large workings to move life-size human or monster models, while those fitted with other mechanisms could not only make comedic faces, but could spit fire or climb trees as well. But none of these techniques could begin to compare to the manipulations that'd played out on the ferry, which could almost be called a sort of sorcery.

Quietly crushing the doll of the hirsute warrior under foot, Glen turned in D's direction.

It would've been nice to say Glen was every bit as handsome as the Hunter, but ultimately his good looks were still of this world. They were a far cry from the inhuman beauty that radiated from D. Around him alone the dusky sky and sea seemed tinged with an unearthly glow.

"Did you think you'd shaken me?" asked Glen. "Sorry to disappoint you, but I've been following you for a week. And once you'd come this far, it was pretty obvious where you were going. I wanted to let you think I'd given up so I could actually go on ahead of you, and it looks like you fell for it."

"Why are you following me?" D asked.

"Because you made me flinch," Glen replied, a bitter smile rising on his lips.

"Flinch?"

"That night. That was the first time I was ever afraid of anyone. I couldn't even cross swords with you. And that's why I'm here."

"What do you plan on doing?" asked D.

"Cutting you down," Glen said matter-of-factly. And yet, there was a certain repulsiveness to his declaration that sent an involuntary shudder down the woman's spine.

Suddenly, the wind whistled. The waves broke, one after another.

Glen's voice fit the mood perfectly. "I'll cut you down with my own two hands. I won't be able to live with myself until I've done so."

Saying nothing, D turned his back toward the man and his intense gaze.

"I won't do it here," Glen said, his words following after the Hunter. "But someday—at the right time, in the right place. Now, don't run off on me."

D's left hand hung at ease by his side, and from it came the words, "Sounds like this guy was born to fight. Oh, what a pain."

But in the end, that hoarse voice never reached Glen's ears.

III

"Hey, wait up!" the woman called out to stop D on the squalid aft deck, which was crowded with horses and wagons and all sorts of strange baggage. "I can't believe I ran into not one but two incredibly powerful guys. So, where were you—" the woman began to ask, but then her lips formed an awkward smile. "Oh, there I go asking a traveler the stupidest question. From the look of it, I don't suppose I could even begin to guess where you're going. It's just that I was sort of curious."

"Why is that?"

The woman's eyes went wide. She never could've imagined this young man having any interest in anyone else.

"Because I helped you out?" the Hunter asked.

There was that, of course. She didn't know whether she should be elated or horrified by the skill the young man had displayed in keeping the spear-man from attacking. However, in addition to that—

The woman shook her head from side to side, a weary look on her face. "No," she replied. "But that reminds me—I haven't expressed my gratitude yet. Thank you. My name's Su-In."

"I'm D."

"That's a great name. It's like a sadness in the wind," Su-In said, suddenly breaking into a smile.

It was a strange reaction. Those who met D's beauty face to face and felt his strange aura were shaken by an unholy emotion that went hand-in-hand with their lust. They saw the Noble in him. But this woman alone seemed to be an exception. As she gazed at the dark huntsman, her eyes seemed to hold a boundless feeling of nostalgia.

The wind whistled.

Shivering, Su-In clasped her collar shut with one hand. "My, but it's cold. If you were to tell someone from down south that this is summer, I don't think they'd ever believe it."

The woman turned toward the sea. The shadowy form of land was growing more substantial—but in front of it there bobbed a whitish lump—a chunk of ice. This was the northern sea, after all.

The weather controllers set beneath all of the continents hadn't been able to stand ten millennia without adjustments, and the humans' destruction had extended to even those devices once thought impregnable. As a result, in certain areas the course of nature was disregarded, and even now the seasons continued to follow a bizarre pattern. For example, near the center of this seven-mile-wide waterway the air and water temperatures suddenly plunged. No ice could be seen from the dock, but halfway across the chunks quickly became more and more common. While this was completely natural for those who lived in the area, the vast majority of travelers and merchants visiting for the first time would huddle in the ship and come down with a cold.

"Every time I travel these waters, I get the feeling summer's never gonna come again," Su-In said, the words rushing out like a sigh. Her breath formed white crystals.

"There's something I'd like to ask you," said D.

"Whatever it is, kindly ask away."

"Where did you learn to do what you did?" D asked. He must've seen her fighting the man with the spear.

Not faltering in the least, Su-In replied, "When I was a kid, my village hired warriors. There was a lot of trouble back then. I guess I was a quicker study than any of the other girls."

"Most men couldn't have done that, either."

"Stop it. You're embarrassing me," Su-In said, smiling wryly. There was no feminine fawning in her smile. Apparently, one of this woman's strong points was being as guileless as a blue autumn sky. "You know, even without that my reputation is bad enough, what with people always calling me a tomboy or saying I could blow away a mechanized beast just by sneezing. So I'll thank you to choose your words with care."

"I will."

"Stop it already. Would you just drop the serious face?" Su-In said, putting her hands out before her as if disgusted. "When I look at you, I feel like I can't say anything until I dig up some deep philosophical point to discuss. Why don't you try lightening up a bit?"

"Been like that since birth."

Su-In's eyes bulged in their sockets. The facetious reply had come in such a hoarse tone it was hard to believe it could possibly belong to the young man before her. Scanning the surrounding area in amazement, her eyes had a dubious look in them when they came back to D. "Did you just say that?" she asked.

"You bet—" the strangely fascinating tone replied, but it was suddenly choked out by a muffled cry of pain.

This time Su-In was staring at D's left hip, and after her eyes fell on his tightly clenched left hand, she looked up at the man's lovely face and asked, "So, are you a ventriloquist or something?"

"Well, sort of," the same voice replied.

"Aren't you a man of many talents!" the woman exclaimed, her face brimming with admiration.

Once again clenching his fist disinterestedly, D gazed toward land as he said, "We'll be there soon."

The ferry dropped anchor precisely on schedule, and family members and hotel touts were there to greet the disembarking passengers. Only slightly larger than the one on the opposite shore, this dock echoed with a wild mix of voices and footsteps. Though this was the first ferry of the afternoon, the sky remained dark, and it seemed like dusk couldn't be that far off. Even the shadows people cast on the quay were thin.

Across the street was a line of brightly colored roofs. All of the homes were made of stone. Out on the Frontier, where one gust of the cold wind could freeze you to the bone, it was said to be the best sort of insulator. Behind the stone houses was a black mountain range projecting into the melancholy darkness of the sky. The colors worn by the people coming and going on the street were equally dark and oppressive.

Spotting a bus station soon after leaving the dock, D walked over to the barrack-style office with his cyborg horse and asked which way it was to the village of Florence.

He was told he'd have to make his way out of the north end of town, and then go over a mountain. The official grew pale as he also advised the young man not to go after sundown. "The area around the village used to be crawling with Nobility. Even now, there're plenty of odd happenings in those parts at night. And the lone bus that'll go there only runs in the daylight."

Leaving the office, D quickly got back on his horse. He didn't so much as glance at the people coming out of the landing. Undoubtedly Glen was out there somewhere, with his gaze pinned on the Hunter.

With a piercing screech, an engine-driven truck stopped right next to him. Though the empty cargo bed of the truck was wide open, the front seat was enclosed by iron plates. The door opened with a loud creak of its hinges, and Su-In stuck her head out.

"I suppose this is good-bye," she said, her cheeks as rosy as apples thanks to the chilly air.

"Where are you headed?" D asked her. Perhaps he had some sort of hunch what she was going to say.

"Florence."

"Live there, do you?" asked the Hunter.

"That's right."

"I hear the roads are dangerous by night," was all D said as he tugged at his reins.

"How did you know that?! Say," Su-In called out to him, somewhat flustered, "if you're going that way, at least let me go along with you. As it happens, the road splits in quite a few places, and when it comes to dealing with strange characters, I've got more experience. The fact is, I'm in a hurry, too."

"If you slow me down, I'll leave you behind."

"Funny—I was about to say the same thing to you," Su-In shot back, letting her white teeth show.

From beside her, someone else commented in an austere tone, "I'll forever be in your debt," and bowed without looking at D. It was the same traveling holy man who'd stepped in to stop the fight between Su-In and the bald warrior back at the other landing.

"He helped me out when there was trouble back at the dock. Said he came to spread the word hereabouts, and that he'd love to go see Florence, too."

"Well, I'm leaving right away."

"So am I," Su-In replied, a confident grin on her lips. As she sat behind the wheel of the truck, it was as if the simple country girl had become an entirely different person.

Just as the cyborg horse's iron-shod hooves tore into the ground, the truck's gasoline-powered engine gave a mighty roar.

Five minutes after leaving town, they came to a steep mountain road. The narrow lane that seemed to creep across the mountainous terrain disappeared between the trees.

Su-In stopped her truck. "Care to live a little dangerously?" she asked D.

"How's that?"

"The regular way is to the right. But that'll take us till noon tomorrow. If we go this way, we'll get there by morning," she said, her pale finger indicating the slope before them.

At first glance, it didn't seem like much more than an area densely overgrown with trees and weeds, but a closer look through the faint darkness revealed an almost metallic glint barely discernible between the bizarrely twisted stalks and leaves. Apparently it was a road.

"This was the Nobility's road. It punches straight through the mountain and runs all the way to Florence. As a matter of fact, the road we've been using up till now is part of the same one; it's just been covered with dirt. Folks tried to get rid of it, but even a pile of gunpowder couldn't put so much as a little bitty crack in it. I suppose the Nobles' vehicles could've driven there in two hours, but we'll be lucky to get there by morning. Yeah, I know it looks like hell, but once you're on it, the bushes and trees don't really get in the way much."

"Good enough," D said, wheeling his horse around. A second later, he raced ahead. The truck sped off just a little behind him.

Just as Su-In had promised, the grass and shrubs weren't much of a hindrance at all. The iron-shod hooves rang out loudly on the road. Though various shades of green hid either side of the road, it had to be easily thirty feet wide. It was constructed of a reinforced plastic—undoubtedly, this highway had been intended exclusively for high-speed cars. In ages past, robotic horses and electronic cars designed to resemble elegant carriages would've passed this way bearing the lords and ladies of the Nobility. But all of that had become mere dreams of distant days, and now the hooves of a Vampire Hunter's mount and the sickly rattle of an engine echoed across it.

They continued down that road for perhaps two hours. The world had already surrendered itself to the mastery of darkness, and yet there wasn't a moon or even a single star to be seen in the stagnant heavens. It was just the sort of dark night that robbed all who dwelt on the Frontier of any peace of mind.

Off in the distance, there was the howl of what sounded like a wolf.

Rider and truck traveled side by side, with the vehicle's headlights throwing bright circles on the road ahead as they zipped along at around forty miles per hour.

Suddenly the old priest turned to the woman in the driver's seat and said, "My word, the aura of the supernatural has gotten thick out here. It certainly is a comfort having *him* along with us," he groaned, the most solemn of expressions on his face.

"It sure is. He's a hell of a man. I bet he could take this mountain road without any light at all."

"In this pitch black? He couldn't possibly . . ." the priest said, his words dying out. But he soon gave a nod of acceptance— even he must've been able to see the power within the young man who rode alongside them. "Who on earth is he? The other man back at the dock was certainly good looking, but he couldn't begin to measure up to this one for sheer other-worldliness. Seems like he might have some blood that's not entirely human . . ."

"Could be."

"Lowly wretch that I am, I did happen to see a picture postcard of your village back in Cronenberg. It really is quite a nice—"

"Look out!" Su-In shouted.

The vehicle's rubber-wrapped wooden wheels squealed harshly, and the priest went nose-first into the windshield.

Catching a glimpse of something moving out of the corner of her eye, Su-In leaned out the window. "D, what was that just now?" she asked.

Something white had cut right through the bright ring of the truck's headlights. Judging from the fact that he'd halted his horse, D had clearly seen it, too.

"It was human in form," said D. He was gazing off to the same side of the road where it had disappeared.

"In form?"

"I could see right through it. Probably a phantasm or some kind of holograph. You wouldn't happen to know anything about it, would you?"

"It seems this used to be a hunting ground for the Nobility. Maybe it's a ghost."

"I couldn't say for sure. And I don't have time to look into it. Let's go."

Nodding, Su-In said, "You're decisive. I like that." She sounded quite charmed.

Once more they raced off into the darkness, and another hour passed.

Still holding a handkerchief to his brow as he leaned forward in his seat, the priest said, "Hey, that looks like—"

"A tunnel," Su-In said.

Ahead of them, a glowing half-moon shape was rapidly drawing nearer.

"But there are lights burning inside!"

"Well, that's because it was built by the Nobility," the woman replied. "This road is over ten thousand years old, you know."

Neither D nor Su-In halted. In no time, hoofbeats echoed all around them. Then they stopped. Su-In slammed on the brake as well.

The road seemed to run on forever in a straight line, but out in the middle of it a lone figure was simply standing. It was a man garbed in a blue cape.

Su-In knit her brow.

Something glittered as it fell from the man's body to his feet: drops of water. The droplets rained from every inch of his form, as if he were some drowned soul just pulled from the water. With flowing blond hair, an unwavering gaze, and a regal nose—he had to be a Noble.

For several seconds, no one moved at all. Were they waiting to see how the other would react?

Then there was a harsh clattering. Seeing D galloping into action, the priest gasped. As the Noble stood stock-still, a flash of light from the mounted Hunter blazed toward his neck.

"He vanished!" the priest exclaimed.

At the sound of the old man's voice, Su-In—who was still at the wheel beside him—returned to her senses and a cry of "Huh?!" escaped her.

There was no one on the road D was doubling back over.

"It was just an illusion. There was no substance to it," D said matter-of-factly.

"What do you suppose it was?" Su-In asked him, her voice seeming to cling to him for support. "It was a Noble, right? Never saw one on this road before—I was really scared. But it's been over two hundred years since there were any Nobility around here. I've never heard of there being any vengeful spirits wandering around, either."

Saying nothing, D stared at the spot where the Noble had stood.

The two other pairs of eyes followed his, and at least one of those present let out a cry of astonishment. A glistening stain remained on the semitransparent floor. A puddle of water.

"This is salt water," said D. Su-In didn't see him as he put the palm of his left hand to the puddle. "Sea water . . ." The words were fragmented, but clear. He was contemplating their import.

For a while, there wasn't a single sound.

"Shall we go?" D finally suggested.

"Sure," Su-In responded, her tone already rock-steady once again.

Thirty minutes later they came out of the tunnel—there was forest to either side of them. Between dead trees that looked like the broken fingers of giants were scattered the rotten and collapsed remains of what seemed to be buildings.

"Would you happen to know what those are?" the priest asked with deep curiosity.

"They're said to be vacation homes for the Nobility, but I wouldn't know."

"Oh, so this was some sort of resort then? Even as cold as it is here?"

"It only got like this around here after there was some trouble with the weather controllers. While I've never seen it that way myself, legend has it this area was a tranquil getaway spot, lush and green, thousands of years ago. There are more ruins near the village."

"You don't say."

"All things come to an end, whether they have life or not. See for yourself."

Following the woman's remark, the priest focused on the point she indicated through the windshield and gasped. At some point, the truck and D had been surrounded by pale blue lights. Wolves. Wrapped in a dazzling phosphorescence, dozens of them raced all around the truck and horse. From their eyes spilled streaks of flame, and from their savagely rent lips came gouts of burning blue breath.

"Oh, this isn't good at all!" the old priest cried. "Those are pets of the Nobility—'Children of the Night.' Nothing on earth savors the taste of human flesh more than these creatures!"

"Get a grip on yourself. You're not very enlightened for a priest, are you?" Su-In said scornfully. "They're all illusions. The real pets died off ages ago."

"Well, I'll be!" the priest said, breaking into a grin and lightly smacking himself on the cheeks. Laughing aloud, he claimed he'd suspected it was something like that all along.

Su-In then said to him, "But they sure act like you'd expect pets of the Nobility to. Even though they're just illusions, they still go after humans. Listen to that."

The sound of trees being shredded shook the holy man's eardrums, leaving him pale as a corpse.

"It's okay. Tough as they are, they can't eat a truck. On the other hand, I wouldn't be so sure about *him*."

"You needn't worry," the priest said, his voice swollen with confidence for some reason.

The luminescent forms were closing on D, too. It was impossible to say whether what gushed from their gaping maws was fiery breath or glowing spittle. One of the beasts was like a speeding ball of light as it came at him with all its might to bite into the horse's right flank. But the very instant it seemed to sink its teeth in, there was a vertical slash of silvery light and the beast's head separated from its body, sailing through the air and vanishing before it could strike the ground.

Two more raced toward the rider this time, blue streaks trailing behind them. Not even bothering to turn, D made a sweep of his sword to the right. As if drawn to the weapon, the vicious beasts launched themselves right into the silvery arc, and were reduced to flecks of light before they vanished. D's skill with a blade was such he could've stopped a foe at the speed of sound.

The wolves' speed dwindled swiftly. D tore right through their midst, and the truck did the same.

After meeting with no other eerie beings, the group reached the exit of the short, final tunnel just as the pale light of dawn was brightening the eastern sky. The Nobles' thoroughfare twisted off into the distance, while to the left of it—beyond the sheer black walls that supported the road—the gray sea lay peacefully. The glittering points near the horizon must've been chunks of ice. The heavens were heavy with clouds the same shade as the sea. Although the distance wasn't quite clear, a thin line that broke off from the white road went on to run along the cliffs at one point, while at the end of it lines of rooftops of some sort of community could be seen. The roofs themselves were all bleak shades quite at odds with the colorful name of Florence.

Though the heater was on in the truck's cab, the priest pulled his collar tight and shivered nonetheless. Su-In had just opened the door and climbed out of the cab.

Looking up at D on his mount, she said, "We're there at last!"

There was no reply.

Long hair billowing out in the chill air that swept in from the sea, the figure of beauty silently gazed at the village that lay ahead. If his eyes could read the whole tale that was about to begin, Su-In thought, the results must be incredibly tragic, and that was enough to leave her frozen in a daze.

The sky, the sea, the wind, and even the young man himself all looked terribly sad.

"Say," the woman began, finally able to speak when the figure on horseback pulled his reins tight, "now that we've come this far, I suppose it should be fair to ask you something. Where are you going in Florence?"

"The home of a girl named Wu-Lin."

Su-In's eyes went wide. "You know her last name?" she asked.

"No."

"What are you going to her house for?"

D turned to Su-In. Not because the intensity of her tone almost made it sound like an interrogation, but because of the way she'd said "her."

"Is she an acquaintance of yours?" he asked.

Never averting her eyes from the young man's bottomless gaze, Su-In said, "Now, this might seem like a terrible thing to say, but that's one name I never wanted to hear from you. Wu-Lin is my little sister."

Gazing at the woman's face for a while, D proffered his left hand in Su-In's direction. It was balled in a fist. He then opened it.

Su-In stared down at the mysterious bead that appeared in the palm of his hand, utterly stunned. "I could see if some other guy had it—but why you?" Su-In asked, tears spilling from her eyes. "My little sister—is she dead, then?"

"Yes," D said, his tone soft but clear. It was as if he were some beautiful messenger for the afterlife. "Her last words were a request that I bring this back to her home. You should take it."

Su-In didn't put her hand out. "So you came all this way to deliver that? Someone like you? I find that really hard to believe. I can't take that from you."

"Why not?"

"Because if I did, you'd turn around right here and be on your way. That's the kind of person you are. Please, just come back to the house with me and tell us about Wu-Lin. You see, I'm actually the one who let her go off to Cronenberg."

The tiniest bit of emotion stirred in D's eyes. Closing his five fingers once more, D pulled the fist back and grabbed his reins.

But the bead didn't fall from his hand. It'd suddenly vanished from his palm.

"Thank you," said Su-In.

As soon as the words had left the woman's mouth, someone behind her said, "No, it's I who should be thanking both of you."

It was the traveling priest, who'd apparently gotten out of the truck at some point. His head was bowed.

"Oh, I'm sorry," he continued. "I've neglected to introduce myself, haven't I? I'm known as Ban'gyoh, which means 'the savage dawn.' I'm also the founder of the Church of the Third Coming. Though to be honest, I should add that it's a new faith with no adherents aside from myself. No money, no followers, and no home at present. All I have is a faith in my beliefs as I travel the wide world, promulgating this new religion. It's been a pleasure meeting you."

And saying that, he promptly turned and started back toward the truck. But on the way, he stopped and looked over his shoulder to say, "And you, sir—though you may appear less than amiable, you must in fact be truly admirable to have come so far to deliver a keepsake. It may well be that you have the blood of God in you. I'm certain someday soon you'll be showered with blessings."

And with that, he went back to the passenger seat of the cab and shut the door.

"That sure is one wacky priest," a hoarse voice declared.

"Huh?" Su-In exclaimed as she looked at D, but naturally she didn't see anyone else there but him.

In no time, the rider and the truck were tearing through the cold wind as they raced on down the white road. The five villains might already be in the village, and the vengeance-seeking warrior Glen was bound to be following the Hunter. And there was no saying if Professor Krolock and the mysterious thief named Toto were still in the game. But what else awaited D here in the northern extreme and the village of Florence?

Village at the Ends of the Earth

CHAPTER 4

I

Soon after entering the village, it became clear that a new day had begun. Inviting smoke rose from chimneys of brick and stone, and there were people out scrubbing dinghies in their cramped yards. Small fish flopped in the streets, and beside every house hung sharp harpoons and nets of flexible steel. The air smelled of salty breezes and fish. Compared to other fishing villages, the slope from the back of the mountains down to the beach was much gentler, and there was quite a bit of level land. The white building that could be spied halfway up the slope appeared to be a weather station, and at the very top of its dome-shaped stone roof a piece of surveying apparatus that looked like an antenna shook in the wind.

Apparently recognizing the truck's owner at a glance, women bundled in fur coats and mufflers and gloves while they repaired nets or poured pots of boiling water on the frozen streets smiled with familiarity toward the vehicle, but as soon as they noticed D they slipped into a daze. In what must've been an attempt to reduce the risks during freezing weather, rubber mats dotted the sloping streets and stone steps. Everyone's breath was white.

Was summer really coming?

Going through the center of town, the group came to a road that overlooked the beach. A short while earlier, Ban'gyoh had gotten out of the truck.

"I am in your debt. May God's blessing be on you!" he'd said, repeating his thanks over and over as he departed.

On a stretch of sand that must've been a mile wide, power boats large and small lay on their sides like strange denizens of the sea's depths. The ships that challenged the freezing seas with anywhere from five to fifty fishermen aboard had high-powered engines one would never expect from their deceptively slow appearance, and they could glide between the icy chunks with the grace of a skater. In a manner of speaking, these ships were the fishing village's advance guard. Apparently under repair, a number of the vessels were suspended by rigging of wood and steel. Waves rolled in from the gray sea their prows still faced, and the wind carried the music of those jostling chunks of ice.

Suddenly, D shifted his gaze inland.

Following his eyes, Su-In found the elevated stage that could be glimpsed through the grove of evergreens. "That's the band tower for the summer festival," she said. "They'll be having it back there pretty soon. There'll be dancing and concerts and games—all kinds of stuff."

"Summer?" said D.

"Yeah," Su-In said with a nod, a faraway look in her eyes. "Even way up north in a dead little village like ours, summer still comes around, you know. And when it does, we have our celebration." A hint of expectation skimmed across the face of the same woman who'd earlier muttered her own doubts about whether summer was coming. "It'll be here in just three days. Out on the Frontier, summer might come to different places at different times, but ours will be here in three days."

Having followed the shore road for half its length before turning right, Su-In's truck then ran alongside a broad drainage ditch for five minutes before it halted. The west side of the stone house was

MYSTERIOUS JOURNEY TO THE NORTH SEA PART ONE | 89

enveloped in steam—this was because the water running down the side of the street was actually boiling hot. No doubt it was the result of a water-heating system somewhere.

A gray-haired old man who must've heard the truck's engine came out of the front door dragging one leg behind him as Su-In pulled onto the property.

"Allow me to introduce you. This is my grandfather, Han. Grampa Han, this is Mr. 'D.' He's been kind enough to come all this way with a message from Wu-Lin."

The old man had a harsh glint in his eye as he looked D over, but he soon broke into a smile. "Welcome! Any friend of my granddaughter's is a friend of mine. Come on, now. Step right inside and don't be shy!"

Once they were in the living room, the chill had dissipated. The hot water running down the side of the street also circulated through the stone walls and floors to heat them, and the insulating properties of the rocks themselves now served to hold the warmth very well. Su-In and the old man seemed mesmerized by the bead D placed on the table with his left hand. After hot coffee was set out and Grampa Han had been informed of Wu-Lin's demise by Su-In, the old man didn't say anything for some time.

"And she died because of that bead?" Su-In finally ventured.

"Most likely."

"Who killed her?"

"The same kingpin back in town that hired the man we met on the ship and his colleagues. Gilligan was his name."

"And what's he doing now?"

"He's dead."

Su-In stared at D. "You paid him back for my sister, didn't you?"

"I suppose you could say that."

"Why? Now, I don't know what line of work you're in, but by the look of you I take it you're a warrior or a Hunter. Did my sister hire you then?"

"Gilligan wasn't a Noble."

Su-In's eyes stretched wide with surprise. "So, you're a Vampire Hunter . . . Come to mention it, I'd heard there was one out on the Frontier so good-looking it was scary, and that he had an odd name . . ."

"I'll tell you all I know," D said, his coolness slicing through Su-In's astonishment.

When the young man finished giving them the facts, Su-In had her face hidden in her hands. Although no sob escaped her, her shoulders were quaking. Tears fell without end from Grampa Han's eyes, soaking his lap.

"So—I was just wondering if my sister had a peaceful death," Su-In asked, her voice somewhat muffled.

"Yes."

"But she still had enough time to ask you to take care of the bead?"

"Would you have preferred she'd died without saying anything?" asked the Hunter.

"That's not—"

"Of course she wouldn't have wanted that," the old man said.

"We're not going to get her body back, are we?" said Su-In.

"No, but she still looked so lovely."

"Thank you."

"I'm done here. Thanks for the coffee," D said as he got to his feet.

"Wait," Su-In called out to stop him. "Are you just going to leave?"

"My business here is finished."

"Terrifying people are headed toward our village to get this bead. Worse yet, they're probably already here. Please—you've got to fight them."

"Give them the bead. No matter what its value may be, it's not worth more than your life."

"I just can't do that. Not after my sister gave it to you at the cost of her own life!"

"I only deal with Nobility."

If D had seriously made the remark in an attempt to leave, you could say it was a grave error. Su-In's eyes sparkled. Maybe they were saying that she'd successfully trapped him, or perhaps they were just filled with the purest hope.

"There's Nobility in this village, too," she said, staring fixedly at D's face.

"This is the first I've heard of it."

"It's a big skeleton in the village's closet, and they don't exactly let it get out. Just knowing there was Nobility here would be enough to keep folks from buying our fish."

In the Northern Frontier, hatred of the Nobility was especially strong. In extreme cases, it wasn't unheard of for an entire town to pick up and move when someone simply discovered a few of the Nobility's ruins there. And that was nothing compared to what they'd do if the accursed creatures were actually prowling around again—

"What kind of Nobility?" the Hunter asked.

"I'll tell you that in a minute. Wait. I want to put the bead away first."

Su-In got up and went into one of the back rooms, returning a short while later.

"Where did you stash it?" Grampa Han asked as he wiped away his tears.

"In the usual box," Su-In replied casually.

Just then, there was an urgent knock at the door.

"Wonder who that could be at this hour?" Getting to her feet again, Su-In walked over to the intercom beside the door. Coughing once, she asked, "Who is it?"

"It's me—Dwight!" a man said, his rough voice carrying a strange tension. "I raced right on over here just as soon as I heard you were back. Just a little while ago, your grandfather's body washed up in 'the jaws' by the cape."

"Don't talk nonsense—" Su-In shot back, but even as she said these words something struck her and she turned toward her grandfather.

Grampa Han was on his feet. He was probably going to make a break for it.

But that wasn't the way it went. Right in front of him, a disturbing streak of light raced from left to right. As he looked at D and the blade he held, the old man's eyes swam with hatred and fear.

"That's quite a disguise," said D. "Are you one of the five Gilligan sent?"

"Oh, you know about us, do you?" the old man replied, his fearful tone suddenly becoming more vibrant and youthful. "I'm known as 'the Indiscernible Twin.' I've had a bad feeling ever since I found out you were the Vampire Hunter D. Tell me something—when did you know?"

"When you asked where she'd put the bead."

Grampa Han—or rather, Twin—scratched at his gray beard and said, "Sheesh, that was careless of me. But I was so sure of my disguise."

"So it was you that killed her grandfather then?"

"It sure was. Wouldn't do to have two of us running around, would it? But after all the trouble I went to disguising myself as her grandfather so I could get all kinds of info out of her before I did her in, in comes this major hurdle."

Rooted by the vile and stunning confession she'd just heard, Su-In reflexively undid the bolt when she heard another frantic knock on the door.

The young man who flew in had the imposing build of a grizzly bear. Even through his heavy leather coat and trousers the contours of his muscles stood out starkly. A pair of foot-long wooden clubs connected by a leather strap were stuck through his belt. "Morning," he grunted to Su-In as he raised a hand in greeting, but after he caught a glimpse of the situation in the living room over the woman's shoulder, his eyes bulged in their sockets. "What in the world?! But you're—"

"He's an impostor!"

"What?! An impostor?!"

"I thought she told you we were busy in here," Twin said with a wink of his right eye to Dwight, and then he reached out in a smooth motion and grabbed hold of D's sword with one hand.

Although the blade didn't look like it moved at all, it was D's skill alone that left all five of the old man's fingers scattered across the floor.

"Damn, that hurt!" the old man said with a grimace. "But it looks like that's what it's going to take to get me out of here," he added as he leapt back. He was still in midair when something black spouted from his right shoulder. A second later, the old man's body made an impossible bound for the window and disappeared, leaving only the sound of breaking glass behind.

Shouting, "Hold it, you bastard!" Dwight jumped right out after him.

Not entirely sure what'd just happened in the wake of these incredible events, the dazed Su-In looked at D and noticed his eyes were intently scrutinizing his own blade. "D . . ." she said.

Not responding, D brushed the blade of his sword with his left hand.

His masterful swordplay should've left the foe who called himself Twin split in half through the clavicle and scapula. But halfway through, it had made no more progress.

There was a strange feeling in his fingertips. About a foot and a half from the tip, something semi-translucent, like a thin film, adhered to his blade. Peeling it off, he found that it was indeed a thin, gelatinous membrane. Dripping with viscous goo, layer upon layer of this membrane had wrapped around the Hunter's blade, leaving it too dull to cut at all. There was no need for him to wonder where his foe might've kept such a substance. Undoubtedly it was part of Twin's very own skin.

As D sheathed his sword without saying a word, Dwight returned.

"He's long gone. Jumped into the flume by the street. You have any idea how hot that water gets? It's gotta be boiling—that bastard dove right in like it was nothing. Goddamn freak!" With the same anger that his voice had carried now in his eyes, the young man stared at D. "And who the hell's this?"

"I was going to introduce him to you later—this is Mr. D. He ran into Wu-Lin down in Cronenberg and was good enough to bring us a message from her. He's a warrior."

At Su-In's reply, the young man grew visibly angry. "Great! Only the worst kind of musclebound drifter. All of a sudden we've got all kinds of freaks pouring into town. Well, they're not exactly invited to the summer festival."

"Now, don't say things like that. He's here because I asked him to come."

At Su-In's firm tone, Dwight's mouth became a tight-lipped frown and he held his tongue. It wasn't that Su-In had got the better of him—there seemed to be some other special reason. "Yeah, well, what the hell's going on here?" he asked. "I mean, what are you gonna do? About your grandfather's body, that is."

"I'll be right over to pick him up. I'm sorry, but you'll have to leave now."

Once Dwight had left with a sullen look on his face, Su-In stood there with a pitiful expression.

"I—I'm all alone now," the girl mumbled, and as she took a step, she staggered. A fit of dizziness had swept over her. Any ordinary man or woman would've had the soul torn out of them by the series of tragedies and strange events she'd been through. But her shoulders were supported by cold, strong hands.

"You'd better take the bead with you," D said softly. "All of *them* must know where your house is."

Su-In looked back at D like a floundering student who'd just been given encouragement by a focused instructor. Her deep brown eyes instantly filled with tears—and hope. "Will you stay here with me?" she asked.

"Are you going to hire me?"

"Sure," Su-In replied with a forceful nod. She wasn't crying anymore.

"My compensation will be the bead."

Su-In's expression reflected surprise for a moment, but she nodded her assent to his condition. "I'll leave everything to you, then. If I give it to you, I'll be safe. Thank you."

Returning to the room in the back of the house, Su-In got the bead and handed it to D.

The two of them went outside.

The glow of dawn had become the heavy light of morning.

II

Desolate in some indefinable way, the strangely spacious chamber nevertheless retained touches here and there of an otherworldly grandeur. Although outside the vitality of morning had become a light that filled the world, a single shadowy figure came into this place where murkiness yet lingered.

"I smell blood," said a female voice from somewhere in the darkness.

A few hazy figures could be seen there if you stared hard enough, and though you could definitely make out a fair bit of the intricate carving on the chairs and sofas and tables, the occupants remained mere silhouettes. However, it was the same feminine voice that'd echoed from one of the doorways back in Gilligan's outbuilding.

"You were beaten, weren't you? Not as tough as you made yourself out to be," someone sneered in a grave tone from a heavily draped window.

"I can't say that I blame you. I'm in no position to laugh, you know," said a third voice. It was clearly that of "Shin the Manipulator."

At this point the fourth and final speaker would've been expected to say something, but oddly enough, only the same low, beastly growl heard back at Gilligan's suddenly rolled from one side of the chamber.

"I blew it," Twin said, not sounding the least bit daunted as he seated himself on the floor in the middle of all the other speakers. Not surprisingly, only the vaguest outlines of his face and body could be seen—no doubt these were the conditions under which they'd all agreed to meet. "I disguised myself as the old man and went there in the hopes of getting the stone and all its secrets from the girl. I'd gotten the geezer to tell me his granddaughter had gone down to Hanbury to buy the latest kind of whetstone, so I was just sitting around biding my time when she came back with a house guest from hell. He was—"

"D," Shin interrupted in a tone that sent chills down their spines.

"I was pretty sure that's who it was. My skin veil managed to slow his blade, but I'm still a mess. Another fraction of an inch and he'd have cleaved me to the bone. There wasn't a thing I could do about it—just say thanks and bye-bye. And on top of everything else, I wound up getting soaked in boiling hot water. The world's not a complete loss yet if there're still scary characters like him around . . ."

"Was it someone else that took out Shin?"

"I wasn't taken out. I just lost an arm."

"Shin, when did you get back?" asked Twin. "I was sure you must've died along the way or something. You've got a lot of nerve slinking back here and joining up with the rest of us."

"Don't say that," said the deep voice that interceded. "As luck would have it, I happened to see him on my way here and I asked him to come along. At any rate, he's agreed to join forces with all the rest of us so we can bring the bead back together."

"Speaking of that," the woman's voice interrupted, "we left it to Twin to get the thing because we thought there was just an old man and a girl guarding it and it'd be foolish for all of us to be fighting each other to get to it first. But now it appears we should start looking out for ourselves again. Whoever takes out her bodyguard should be first in line for it, I say."

"I don't think so," Shin said in a low voice.

"That's because he put the fear into you," the woman sneered.

But someone else came to his aid, saying, "I don't think so, either." He meant that he agreed with Shin—it was Twin. "It might rub you folks the wrong way, but it'd be a lot safer if we all took him on at once. Underestimate him and you'll only meet a quick death."

"I'll try to ignore your lack of experience, but kindly refrain from making such broad pronouncements," the woman said, her voice like a thorn—a thorn dripping with poison. "At any rate, our little pact of unity is at an end. I'm going to do as I please," she added.

"Me, too," the owner of the deep voice concurred. He then asked, "What'll you do, Gyohki?"

There was no immediate reply, but after a while a strangely lisping and panting answer came. "I'll claim it all. His life, the bead—everything."

"Then it's decided," said the man—who could only be Egbert.

"How interesting! Don't come complaining to us if one of the others bumps you off, Twin and Shin." Laughing, the woman added, "That leaves just the boy and the old man. Perhaps you can sit around and discuss your retirement. But let me make it perfectly clear that if either of you even thinks of pulling something before we're done—"

"I know, I know," Shin said. "We won't try anything until you've taken him out of the picture. That is, *if* you can take him out."

"This should be rich!" said Twin, his subsequent laughter rocking the room. "Okay, give it your best shot. Once the rest of you are done, me and Shin will move in. At least try to leave a few marks on him, will you?"

"Well, shall we go? We can leave word back here."

And with that solemn voice as a cue, every last sound ceased. It was evident that all five of the villains had flown from their meeting place without letting any of their compatriots ever see them, and each embraced their own dangerous thoughts.

Although the dull sunlight dribbled through the clouds in the late afternoon to illuminate every last corner of the village, the air and wind remained sharp enough to cut into the flesh. But that same chill air rang high and low with a jubilant pounding and the sound of hammers making preparations for the summer festival, which was set to begin in a few short days.

D and Su-In heard the ruckus from the top of the truck as they headed toward the shops in town. Because the engine was acting up, the truck was being pulled by a pair of cyborg horses. It was hard to imagine that summer would be there soon—despite the fact that it was already in full swing in many other parts of the Frontier. Nevertheless, the sounds of the work seemed to stir up that summertime feel.

Su-In sat beside D as he held the reins, and her face was as dark and gray as the sea. At the moment, she was headed out to buy the things she'd need for her grandfather's funeral and to file the paperwork for his death certificate. The cause of death was drowning, but they knew who'd arranged for it to happen. Ordinarily, that was information they'd give to the sheriff. But it was Su-In's decision not to do so. The enemy was after a single bead. Getting others involved would only cause her more misgivings, and with the festival so close, there was reason to fear the trouble could spread through the whole village. The sheriff would be certain to request the assistance of the Vigilance Committee and the Youth Corps. Relying only on D and herself, Su-In was determined that the two of them alone could meet the threat posed by their attackers when they came.

The real problem was Dwight, but she'd eventually persuaded him. Not only was he head of the local Youth Corps, but he'd known Su-In all her life and was madly in love with her. When she'd asked him not to mention it to anyone else, he'd become belligerent. But a threat of never having anything to do with him ever again finally got his grudging consent.

However, there was no guarantee that word wouldn't get out eventually—it was a small village. Strange rumors got around quickly, and when the woman had gone to pick up the remains, there was certainly somebody that'd seen D with her and was certain to start whispering about it. Though she'd introduced him as an acquaintance of Wu-Lin's who'd be working for her for a while, it was too much to expect even the simplest rustic to believe a woman who'd barely turned twenty would be taking in a gorgeous young man with an eerie aura as an ordinary laborer. All she could do was accept that some loss of reputation and a certain amount of talk behind her back were unavoidable.

Her grandfather's corpse was brought back to their barn, and the doctor raced over to examine it. The wake would be that night, and the funeral was the following day.

Coughing with the cold air as she breathed in, the woman suddenly felt relief and warmth shining into her heart like a thin ray of sunlight, thanks to simply having D there silently driving the vehicle. It wasn't something the average person could've made her feel. So beautiful he seemed shaped by a genius or by the heavenly creator himself, his body shrouded in a daunting aura, so cultured he seemed like a Noble—as they were going to get her grandfather's remains, she'd wanted him to make it clear he was actually a dhampir, but there was something about the elegant form of this young man in black that was far beyond the ken of ordinary people like herself. There was something entirely different about him.

His form was as human as Su-In's own, but he was steeped in an air of mystery beyond her or any other human's imagining—an air that could be felt merely by being near him. For that very reason, many dhampirs didn't let anyone else get close to them. Warriors and bodyguards who traveled around selling their services were the same way. Su-In knew just from those who'd visited the village in the past that they had what could almost be called a stern disregard for everyone else. While this young man proved far more solitary and aloof than the others had been, for some reason the mere thought of him by her side brightened her psyche, which was otherwise ready to plunge into despair, and made her feel she might just be able to go on another day.

"Have you settled down some?"

Finding herself on the receiving end of this abrupt query, Su-In hurriedly focused herself back on the present. "Yeah. Somewhat."

"Now that I'm working for you, could you tell me the story behind the bead?"

"Sure," Su-In replied with a nod, gazing out at the vast expanse of sea to her right. "Most of what I know I heard from my grandfather. I already told you this whole area used to be a hunting ground for the Nobility, right? That was over a thousand years ago. Back in those days, it seems even the northern Frontier was managed by the weather controllers, and they could make it warmer or pleasantly cool. The Nobles' homes—or rather, their lodges—weren't just in the woods we passed through last night; they covered the whole area around here. If we hadn't turned toward the village on that road last night but kept going straight, we would've come to the spot where the most extravagant homes were. There's not much to see there now, but it's more than enough to convey how lavish it must've been way back when. Rumor has it that there are underground factories out there still running.

"Do you know what the Nobility did when they wanted to play here? They went sailing on yachts powered by wind or by light waves, or went walking through the sea in submersible spheres. If you go out around the cape, you can still see the remains of an undersea observatory. But the cruelest and craziest thing they did was to cause widespread mutations in the sea creatures. They scattered food and drugs designed to alter the animals' DNA over thousands of nautical miles. For the Nobility, it was a simple enough task. Even now you can go to the room of records at the temple and see data captured by the Nobility back then, although it's forbidden to call up any of the holographic images they have. You see, a number of people have been driven mad by them.

"I've only seen photos myself, but there were some incredible things—it's almost impossible to believe there were ever things like that in our own sea. Giant stingrays that were each six miles wide, barracudas that could swallow three white whales whole . . . When you think of plankton, nothing comes to mind but whale food. But after the Nobility got their hands on them, they were huge, ravenous monsters that could take a big school of seven-foot tuna right down to the bone. There's this one picture where the whole sea—out to the horizon, or even further—is just covered with them. The Nobility used to get into transparent globes that no tooth could even scratch and drink their wine as they watched these creatures tearing into each other. I suppose you know what their wine was flavored with."

"And have humans lived here ever since?" D asked. His tone hadn't been affected at all by the horrible tales he'd just heard.

"It seems they were brought here at the same time the Nobility opened their resort. All the manual labor was done by robots, but it appears that for some of the finer touches they just couldn't beat human servants. Having more obedient human servants than anyone else was quite a status symbol for the local Nobility. The humans had a number of other uses as well. I'm sure you know all about *that*, too.

"After a while, the Nobles took all the humans except for a few servants and put them in one place. And then, after giving them the least amount of support possible, they began preying on their former slaves each and every night. In other words, their greatest joy came from draining the blood from humans who fought back. It turns out they'd realized how boring it was to bite into the throat of humans they kept locked up in dungeons or ones who did their every bidding thanks to sorcery or brain surgery. Making it so that the humans couldn't leave the area they'd been assigned was child's play for the Nobility. And they just left the humans they'd fed on right there. They'd be found by their fellow humans, who'd hammer a stake through the victim's heart—one theory has it that the Nobility derived their greatest satisfaction from hearing that pounding and those screams as they closed the lids to their coffins. Whenever the population fell, they could always have as many humans as they liked sent from the Capital. According to the records, it seems that over the course of a decade, the community was completely emptied five times.

"I'm sure you've seen with your own eyes the beauty and magnificence of the civilization the Nobility left behind. Exquisite gardens that glittered in the moonlight, dreamily blazing torches soaked in perfume, lodges built of silver birch and crystal, and people in white dresses and black capes roaming the cobblestone streets with neither a sound nor a shadow—why would any species that'd learned to live in such splendor need to drink the blood of humans? When it was time to repaint their vacation homes, why was it the fresh blood of humans they had to use? Why did they have to cut the heads off a thousand people and toss them into the sea to summon their monstrous fish? I wonder if the beauty of a civilization can be completely unrelated to the moral character of the race that created it.

"But one day, an end came suddenly to that age of beauty and cruelty. In no time at all—legend has it it happened over the course of a single night—the Nobility vanished completely. No one knows why. Some scholars attribute it to the weather controller malfunctioning, but it's been proven those problems didn't start until much later. At the very least, it was even later that this area was plunged into freezing cold, which caused the mutated creatures to vanish from the seas and left them choked with icebergs. And that was when humans started living here on their own."

"Aren't there any legends about what happened?" D asked. He was also looking out at the sea.

A number of power boats were skipping across the white waves, leaving thin trails in the water behind them as they moved toward the horizon. Beyond them was the hazy black outline of what seemed to be the back of some creature.

"Part of the Nobility's heritage—a tidal whale," Su-In remarked. "They're seven hundred feet long, and just one of them could support the whole village for six months. We can eat the meat, use the blubber for making wax, insulating coatings, kerosene, and fuel for our cars, and we can use the bones for handicrafts and to make special medicines to treat asthma and scurvy. And 'essence of dragon tongue'—an extract of marine flora and fauna that collects in their intestines—makes a perfume more suited to the Nobility than the housewives who live in the Capital these days. The village will be pretty busy up until the summer festival. I've got to do all that I can, too. D, I'll really need you to watch my back."

Here Su-In took a breath. Closing her eyes, she dug deep into her memories. "This is how the legend goes. One day, a man with more power than even the Nobility came on a ship, brought all the Nobles together in the square, and upbraided them for their cruel misdeeds. When the angry Nobles mounted their battle chariots and charged the man, he not only blew away their war machines but also ripped their very homes from the ground with a single flourish of his cape. It's said that the frightened Nobility, with one exception, all fled the area then."

"And that one exception?"

"His name was Baron Meinster. He was the administrator of this region and the very worst of the Greater Nobility, the blackest cancer Noble blood ever produced—in fact, there are records that show making the sea creatures monstrously large and the 'game' of putting all the humans in one place so the Nobles could feed on them were both his ideas. A truly loathsome portrait of him survived. And letters have been preserved where his fellow Nobles wrote to acquaintances in the Capital, telling them not to go to his home if invited because even Nobility were known to enter and never come out again. At any rate, he alone defied the commands of the mighty traveler. The battle came the day after the other Nobles left, and it took place at Meinster's castle. After a conflict that reduced the homes of the Nobles to rubble instantly, wiped out all animal life, and even changed the shape of mountains, Meinster was defeated and his corpse was cast into the sea for all eternity after measures had been taken to ensure he would never return to dry land again. It's said that even now he prowls the bottom of the deep sea with arms folded, coming up at times to bask in the moonlight and take his sustenance, plotting his return to the land and vengeance against the traveler in black. But that last part is nothing more than legend.

"Oh, that's right—there was one other horrible business Meinster was involved in while he was still alive. Not long after some of the inhabitants disappeared from the community where the Nobles confined them, strange creatures were found in the bay or inlets. The shape of them wasn't entirely human or animal, and they were all shriveled up but still alive, or a torso that still lived without its head, or sometimes it would be the opposite and there'd be just a hand that would grab people by the leg while the severed head was a little ways off gnashing its teeth and screaming for help. All of them still bore some resemblance to people who'd gone missing. You could chop them up and apparently it still wouldn't kill them, but if you put them in the sunlight they'd dissolve. The reason they knew that Meinster was responsible for this was because a number of those people had been seen dragged into his castle. Because the images they'd conjure up were just too horrible, no one ever spoke of what happened up there, but we can guess.

"But thanks to the legendary traveler in black, that never happened again, either. The story goes that after that, he wiped out almost all the sea monsters so that humans could dwell near the shore, and he released the people from the Nobility's control before he left. Ultimately, we never did learn who he was or where he was from. Say, D—you don't suppose he was some relative of yours or something, do you?" Su-In said, gazing at the Hunter's profile with a rare look of childlike mischief in her eyes.

As always, he was cold as steel. And yet, feeling as if she'd said something completely inappropriate, Su-In quickly faced forward again.

Not seeming to mind at all, D said, "Yet there's a Noble here. Is it this Baron Meinster?"

"No, his face is—different."

"When did the attacks start?"

Casting her eyes down, Su-In replied, "Three years ago."

"Who is it, and where does he dwell?"

"I don't know. But—" Su-In continued hesitantly, "well, I can tell you for sure that everyone who's been attacked lived near the beach. Seaweed and salt water were always found at the scene. That's why everyone in the village says . . ."

"It's Meinster's revenge?" D ventured casually. Then, quietly turning to face Su-In, he asked, "It's that illusion we saw in the tunnel, isn't it?"

It took some time before Su-In finally nodded.

III

"But you say it's not Meinster?" the Hunter asked.

"If you'll look at the portrait of him in our records, you'll see."

"And why did he appear to you?"

"It wasn't necessarily me," the woman replied. "It could be he sensed you. And we had that priest with us, too. Nobles have this psychic ability to sniff out their enemies, right?"

"Only a small portion of them."

"Well, I'm sure he's part of that group, then."

"And you say he suddenly showed up three years ago?" said D.

"Yeah."

"Any idea why that is?"

"No."

"What do they say around town?"

"No one has any idea, it seems."

"And has there been anything unusual about the sea?"

Averting her gaze, Su-In said, "Yeah," again. "At the very same time, fatalities tripled out there."

That meant the sea had become three times as dangerous.

"Have protective measures been taken?"

"Only during the summer," the woman told him. "The only time he ever comes is in the week-long period that'll be starting in three days—and that's it. That's all we get for a summer in our village. Do you know of anyplace else with a summer like that?"

"Summer is short everywhere. Always, and for everyone."

"I guess that's true," said Su-In, sounding more like she was talking to herself. "You're right. Anyway, as far as protective measures go around here, the Vigilance Committee and Youth Corps take turns standing watch. They used to dig pit traps on the beach and rig up nets where they thought the Noble might go, but they gave up when all they ever caught was other folks from the village."

"Are the corpses of those who've been bitten disposed of?"

"After they drive a stake through them, they're burnt and the ashes are scattered at sea. I suppose that's not a bad resting place for fisherfolk, though. I hear a really good Vampire Hunter can tell how strong a Noble is just by looking at the wounds. If that's really the case, it's too bad none of them are still here," Su-In said, biting her lip regretfully.

"I don't suppose you know why he only comes in summer."

"No, unfortunately."

"Could you tell me the history of the bead?" D said, tightening his grip on the reins. The coastline had disappeared, and the horse-drawn truck was about to enter the center of town.

"Last summer, he came again. Four people were killed in three days. One really foggy night—and we get a lot of those around here when there's suddenly a huge difference in temperature between the air and the sea—the Vigilance Committee had twice their normal numbers out, but it was no use. The last one was a woman who lived right next door to me. In the middle of the night, around 2:00 Night, her father thought he heard some commotion in her room, but when he knocked on his daughter's door, she didn't answer. As he burst in, a figure in black was just escaping through the window. There was a big racket then, and I raced over as fast as I could. The girl was limp on the bed, and her mother and father were crying and screaming. All of them were as pale as a sheet.

"I could see right away that he'd taken off out the window, so I went after him alone. He'd crossed the street and gone toward the beach, so I knew for sure he must've come out of the sea. As I was on my way down to the shore, he suddenly vanished, and that was the end of it. Still, I searched all over the place, and I was just about to leave because the reinforcements had arrived, and that was when the waves brought something to my feet. It was that bead. I thought about showing it to everyone, but then I felt a bit greedy and decided they didn't really deserve it."

Su-In's eyelashes were trembling. Surely her thoughts had drifted to her younger sister.

"Didn't you try to find out what it really was?"

"No. I just showed it to my grandfather."

"And what did he say?"

"Not a thing. He just got really pale and told me to get rid of it as quickly as I could, and to never touch it again. It started to give me the creeps and I considered tossing it like he said, but then I thought about how lucky I was that it'd washed up right in front of me—I guess I really shouldn't have done that. But I think my grandfather knew something about it. Apparently Wu-Lin asked him some stuff about it too, but he didn't tell her anything. He didn't even seem to like having it lying around."

"Why was it brought to Cronenberg?"

"That's a sore subject," Su-In said, embarrassment showing in her eyes. "You saw the inside of my house, right? We're not so well-off that we could afford to have something lying around that might be worth some good money. My grandfather couldn't get around very well, and Wu-Lin still wasn't able to really pull her own weight yet. There was only so much I could make on my own. You know, a girl wants to be able to at least wear a nice dress in the summer."

"You mean you wanted your sister to have one, don't you?"

"I wanted one, too."

Both of them fell silent. Their vehicle was on a wide thoroughfare. This must've been the shopping center, because the rows of buildings were hung with signs for bars and illustrated placards for what seemed to be gaming centers. There were also a few souvenir shops designed with tourists in mind, and they had roe and dried fish displayed out in front. All had their glass doors shut tight, and their stony walls were laced with a mesh of tiny cracks.

Out in front of the sheriff's office, Su-In got down from the truck. "I think this'll probably take a while," she said. "There's not much to see, but hang around."

Watching as Su-In went through the door, D then leaned back against the wall of the office. He pulled the brim of his traveler's hat down low to fend off the sunlight. Although dhampirs could sleep by either day or night, the blood that flowed through their veins craved rest in the daylight hours. As long as they had to deal with Nobles, that particular characteristic was an extremely useful one.

Several shadows fell at the Hunter's feet. All of them belonged to young men in bulky wool sweaters. Judging from the way they were built, any one of them looked capable of easily wringing the neck of an eight- to ten-foot-long fish.

One of them took a step forward and said, "Working up a sweat, I see, pretty boy." The malice-laden tone belonged to Dwight. "Lucky for us Su-In ain't here. See, there's something I've been meaning to ask you."

D didn't reply. He didn't even bother to look up at them.

Dwight's lips twisted with displeasure.

The men around him stepped forward.

"Hold it. There's only the one of him," Dwight said as he raised one hand to stop the others, then scanned the surrounding street.

Some passersby stopped and began to watch from a distance.

"This ain't really the place for making a racket, either. What say you head over there with me?"

"My employer is in here," D said, still looking down.

"Then my question will keep till later," Dwight said, interlacing his fingers before his chest. With due pretense, he cracked his knuckles loudly. "This village ain't like the Capital or other warm places—it can get a little rough around here. Your average guy wouldn't last half a day. So I'm gonna check you out and see for myself if you've got what it takes. Don't worry—I won't let my buddies lay a hand on you. See, I told them I didn't need them, but they came along anyway. C'mon over here," Dwight said, sticking one hand out with immense confidence. As he winked at the Hunter, he gestured at him to follow. "I'm gonna be bare-handed. Don't go using that sword of yours now."

"Maybe I *will* use it," the Hunter replied.

"Spare me the jokes."

"You trust me, then?"

"If I didn't, you think I'd take you on one-on-one?" Dwight said, holding both his right and left fist out in front of himself. His arms were bent at the elbow, and he swept one fist in an arc as if beckoning his opponent forward. If he ever went to the museum in the Capital, he'd have seen that it was actually an ancient boxing stance. If he'd come up with this technique all by himself, he could be considered quite talented.

D pulled away from the wall. Both arms hanging easily by his sides, he headed over to Dwight. The distance between them closed in no time.

Dwight was a little shaken. He'd been sure the other man was going to keep his distance. Hesitating for a heartbeat to decide whether to back up or respond in kind, he ultimately made the decision unconsciously. The straight he threw at D's face was picture-perfect. His fist was still in midair when he felt something lock around his wrist with incredible strength. The ground and sky switched places, and a heartbeat later his massive form flipped around and his back hit the ground.

"Shit," he groaned, but the way he got right back up again showed he was plenty tough. He hadn't been hurt much at all.

Too close, Dwight berated himself. *Keep some distance and whittle him down. Build up some damage with some light hits, and then when the bastard stops moving, lay him out with the big gun. But first, a little intimidation.*

Dwight glared at D. It was said the mere look he could give people was enough to make him the leader of the Youth Corps. A second later, his whole body was enveloped in a chill that left him paralyzed. There was an unearthly and terrifying aura that emanated from the other man's eyes, freezing his heart, his lungs, and his very bones.

It's those damn eyes, isn't it?!

The instant he realized that, he shut his own eyes and bounded forward in a way that showed his instinct and ability as a veteran brawler. When a sharp pain shot once more through the arms he was swinging blindly, Dwight knew he was beaten. This time the top of his skull took the impact as he was stood on his head and lost consciousness in that same pose.

As D casually made his way back to his spot against the wall, he was surrounded by four more figures.

"That was some freaky shit you just pulled. What the hell are you?!" bellowed a giant every bit as big as Dwight. The single T-shaped claw that curved from the end of his right hand was a gaff hook for landing fish. "Serves that dope Dwight right for showing off. I'm gonna gouge out one of this freak's eyes. We'll have this outsider packing in no time. Heh," he snorted, "looks like we're due for a change in leadership."

At that point he spat at Dwight—who'd finally lost his balance and fallen over onto his stomach—and closed in on D.

In a matter of seconds, keen glints danced to the Hunter's right and his left, before him and behind him. No matter which way he focused his attention, he'd be attacked from the other three directions. It was a skillful ploy.

Each of them saw a flash of white light skim across his right wrist. There was the sound of a blade moving in its sheath on the young man's back. Each screaming curses at him in their heart of hearts, the men swung their arms. But they were oddly light. Something felt wrong about the shape of them, too. Stopping in their tracks, they took a look. Their right hands were gone at the wrist. Blood sprayed wildly from the wounds and rebounded from the ground.

Four screams raced down the street as the afternoon began to take a bluish tinge.

After the cries of pain had streamed past like the tails of a kite, the sheriff came running out of his office. He had a potbelly that made it seem like he must've been raised on nothing but rye whiskey since the day he was born. The oversized revolver he had in his right hand looked as useless as a child's toy. Growing pale at the sight of the blood-soaked quartet writhing in the street, he turned to the people around them and asked, "Who in the hell did this?!"

"He did!" a young man shouted as he pointed to D, who was leaning back against the wall. "I saw it happen, I tell you. He did it!"

"Is that true, fella?" the sheriff asked, sounding somewhat unnerved.

The traveler's hat slowly bobbed up and down.

"Then I've got to take you in. Throw that sword over to me real easy."

"They made the first move on me," the Hunter said.

"That's a lie!" a different man shouted. "I saw the whole thing. The five of them were just walking by, and this guy goes and cuts loose on them out of the blue. Hell, you think one man could take out five if he didn't have the drop on them?"

"You've got a point there. Okay, you over there—go fetch the doctor," the sheriff ordered someone else, and then pointed the barrel of his gun right between D's eyes. "Come with me," he told the Hunter. "If things go badly, we'll have a lynching on our hands."

But then another voice turned the situation around completely.

"You've got the whole thing backwards, Sheriff."

The plump lawman bugged his eyes and said, "But Dwight— you're supposed to be one of the victims here!"

"I'm not a victim or a perpetrator," Dwight replied, staring at D with a strange look in his eye as he rubbed his bull neck. "It was a straight-up fight, plain and simple. Me and the boys picked a fight with him, and he took us up on it. Fair and square, too. He was barehanded against me, but used his sword when the others had their gaffs—and that just plain makes sense. The only thing funny about it was it being four against one."

"Yeah, but still—he went too far. He cut folks' hands off!"

"And what would you have to say if one of those hooks had torn his throat open?" Dwight said as he stood up and knocked the mud from his pants. "You should be thanking him for not taking their heads off. Anyhow, I saw the whole thing from start to finish, even though I was on my head at the time. If the person who started the fight says so, you can't get any more accurate than that. Isn't that what happened, everyone?"

Even though he'd just been laid out, the young man still had the power to cow the onlookers. The men who'd spoken out against D moments earlier had already taken off.

"Looks like no one's got any objections," the lawman remarked. "Oh—here comes the doc. Hurry up and get these boys to the hospital, would you?"

A number of bystanders raced over to the fallen youths and loaned them their shoulders as they helped the wounded up.

"I'll rule this as self-defense. This is your lucky day," said the sheriff. Holstering his gun, he returned to his office.

As Dwight began walking away still shaking his head, a steely voice called out from behind his broad back, saying, "Looks like I owe you one."

"Don't kid yourself," Dwight said as he turned and glared at D. "I just like to do everything fair and square, whether it's fishing or fighting. If you don't play it that way, you go from being a regular guy to being a run-of-the-mill thug. But that don't mean you're done with me yet. Fishermen settle things out on the sea. So you just sit tight till we get around to that, okay?"

"I'll do that."

Taking a couple of steps, Dwight then turned as if he'd just recalled something. "It's just a hunch I have, but I think Su-In's all alone in the world now. I want you to look out for her. See to it she don't get hurt any worse than she's been already."

There was no reply.

As the great bear of a man shuffled off down a road that was slowly taking the blue hue from the sky, the sheriff poked his head out again. To no one in particular he remarked, "That's odd. Su-In's not here."

"What?!" Dwight shouted with a start. "Hey—where's pretty boy?"

Two pairs of eyes peered over to where the Hunter had been, but they met only a vacant stretch of rock wall. Suddenly, all trace of D had vanished from the blue light.

The Figure Behind the Waves

CHAPTER 5

I

S ilently and with a somewhat mournful look on her face, Su-In climbed the slope behind the sheriff's office. When multiple screams of pain sent the sheriff running for the door, Su-In had been ready to get up out of her own seat. It was at that very moment that someone else had appeared between her and the lawman—the sheriff had left without even noticing. An involuntary cry of surprise had nearly spilled from Su-In, but she'd managed to choke it back down.

Wu-Lin?!

The girl who'd died in a distant town was staring at her older sister with the same pretty face she'd had in life. While Su-In knew this couldn't be, such thoughts had already been swept away by a torrent of joy and nostalgia. It was probably only natural that when Wu-Lin headed over to the back door and beckoned to her, the older sister followed along without the least resistance. Her sister opened the door, stepped outside, and closed it again. Su-In repeated the same actions. Of course, she had no way of knowing that she was actually the very first person today to open and close that door.

As if mesmerized by the sadly beckoning Wu-Lin, her sister slipped out the back way and climbed the path up the mountain. There was no sign of anyone else. Before long, she came to a clearing that seemed to be part of a temple's grounds. The surrounding woods only added to the darkness of the approaching night, though what looked like gravestones and the tip of a distant temple could be glimpsed at times through the rows of shadowy trunks. The light that seeped through the gaps in the leaves was almost bluish.

Backed by the verdigris-flecked bronze gates to the temple, Wu-Lin came to a halt. "Now that we're up here, we should be free from interruption," she said.

The voice that came from her cute little lips was that of an unbelievable temptress. And when Su-In heard it, her eyes grew fuzzy, and heartfelt tears rolled down her cheeks.

The beloved deceased—surely both the most fondly remembered and the most difficult thing to resist in the entire mortal world, the very sight of whom made thought and reason crumble. Not only could this sorcery conjure up a realistic image, but it also allowed the user to make the phantasm behave exactly as he or she wished.

The stark white figure that appeared beside the bronze gatepost like a challenge to the twilight was a beautiful woman garbed in dress as pristine as new-fallen snow. Yet as proof that her character was quite the opposite, the blue eyes below her finely shaped eyebrows were charged with an evil and ghostly glow as she stared at Su-In. The woman's lips moved, as did the lips of Wu-Lin, whom Su-In alone could see.

"How fortunate for me that I guessed the murder of your grandfather would eventually bring you to the sheriff's office so I could lay a trap for you there. Nevertheless, that's a fearsome bodyguard you have. I most certainly wouldn't want to confront him directly. I was wondering what I could do when he actually left you easily enough." Chuckling, the woman added, "I really should thank him for that. Now, I have a question for you—where is the bead?"

But in Su-In's mind, it became the voice of her sister, and it sounded like she said, "Where's the bead at anyway? You can tell me, Sis."

Her younger sister would've known where she'd put it, but Su-In was no longer capable of such rational thought. "I gave it to D to hold," she replied.

"That was a stupid thing to do," the woman snapped angrily, but an instant later she smiled. "It matters not who my foe is, though. So long as they live in this world of ours, they must carry someone in their heart they are unable to deny." Chuckling to herself, she added, "And having such a person, they are no match for the power of 'Samon of Remembrances.' Actually, I see this woman has chosen a man to beckon her. Tell me, woman—what is that bead?"

"I really don't know, Wu-Lin," Su-In replied. She saw only the form of her younger sister. However, that wasn't what Samon had just said. She'd said Su-In had conjured up *a man*. At Su-In's reply, Samon tilted her head quizzically. "You called me Wu-Lin . . . and you're not lying. You couldn't be lying. So, I guess you don't know then, do you? Are there any other beads?" she asked the woman.

"No."

"Who knows what the bead really is?"

"No one. No one else in the village even knows it exists."

"Is that a fact?" Samon said, grinning smugly. Wu-Lin smiled as well. "In that case, once I acquire the bead, there'll be no further need for me to remain here. At any rate, I shall use you as bait to get the bead from that stripling Hunter, following which I'll dispose of the both of you. Come!"

Beckoned by her younger sister, Su-In tottered unsteadily toward Samon. Her expression, mired in nostalgia, changed suddenly. Plowing through the haziness of awakening from a dream, memory and reason flooded back into her face.

Samon bugged her eyes. Her spell hadn't failed. And no other external physical phenomenon was responsible either. Nevertheless, it was perfectly clear this woman had emerged from Samon's spell of nostalgia.

Rooted for only a second, Su-In could tell at a glance Samon was her foe, and she then quickly retreated to the stone stairs that led to the temple.

"Who are you?!"

Ignoring the woman's cry, Samon raced closer and tried to grab hold of Su-In's hand. Though she didn't think there was any problem with her power, it was also difficult for her to believe there might be some foe lurking nearby. No sooner did Samon realize Su-In's other hand had come down on the hand grabbing the woman's arm than the sorceress found herself sailing through the air. Astonishment ruined her landing—after turning a somersault, she still landed on her rear.

"Where did you learn that trick?!" Samon snarled, exposing her teeth.

Just then, she heard a calm and scholarly voice in her ear say, *Leave now. And go throw yourself off a cliff somewhere, so you can meet a glorious end. The deep blue sea would be a perfect grave for you. Go now . . .*

Samon would've told herself how ridiculous that was, but her will was rapidly fading. Peace and subservience flooding her heart, the beautiful but wicked warrior easily acquiesced.

The other woman was suddenly stripped of her overwhelming lust for killing and walked off between the trees, but Su-In didn't follow her. Though she sensed she shouldn't take the woman's power too lightly, there was also a deep echo that'd resonated through Su-In's heart at the same time the other woman had turned her back to her.

Don't move, the voice bade her. *Stay just where you are. And listen to me well. Who has the bead?*

D does, Su-In responded, also solely in her mind.

That's right. I heard that, too. This man named D is in possession of your family's precious bead. Now, is that for the best? He's a complete stranger to you, a drifter and a dhampir. He's in league with the Nobility. Do you really think your prized possession is safe with such a man?

He's not like that, Su-In said, refuting the remark with all her might. Somewhere in the universe, someone seemed very surprised.

How strong your conviction! It would seem you've given serious thought to the matter. However, in our youth, everything appears as bright as the sun. Even a figure from the world of darkness. If you would, listen to me well now. And then think. Decide if my words to you aren't the truth, and your own might not merely be prejudiced.

In reality, not a full second had passed since the first word had entered Su-In's head. The words came to her as a mass of condensed information.

After a few more seconds, a gorgeous figure in black raced up the stone steps.

"D?!" Su-In cried, totally forgetting herself as she clung to his powerful chest. But then she pulled back again as if she'd bounced right off him.

"Are you okay?" D asked tersely.

"Yeah. But wait till you hear this."

Su-In then went on to tell the Hunter all about Samon using an illusion of her sister, as well as about the voice in her head. "I don't know why, but the voice was trying to talk me into taking the bead from you. You suppose that woman has managed to get away by now, too?"

"Probably."

"This is beginning to scare me."

"Why don't you just give them the bead then?" D suggested.

"Like hell I will! I dare you to say that again. I'll slap you silly if you ever do."

Saying nothing, D gazed into the woman's eyes.

"But how did you know to find me here?"

"You're better off not knowing."

"Loose lips sink ships, eh? You're sharp, all right," Su-In said, stroking her hair. "It looks like that bead's really valuable, wouldn't you say?"

"So it would seem."

"Well, that just makes me all the more reluctant to let them have it, then," Su-In said with a smile. It was a fearless grin. Such a look normally would've only suited a man's face, but it fit her perfectly now.

The two of them started down the stone steps.

After the pair had disappeared around a corner, an old man whose face was overrun by a beard as white as snow appeared from behind a pillar opposite the gate where Samon had first showed herself. Had he been perusing some heavy tome, he'd have been the very picture of a man of letters, but an air of menace unthinkable from a simple scholar hung all about his cloaked form.

"I've been in town for two days now. So, we meet at last, do we?" Professor Krolock muttered, sounding like he'd finally solved some equation after endlessly wracking his brain. His eyes dropped to the two parchments he gripped in his right hand. Limned in jagged lines, the face of one was no more than a rough sketch—a good rank below the one he'd done of Wu-Lin before—but despite its hasty nature, it definitely captured her character well. "With that first woman, I only had a rough sketch to persuade, but I suppose it should have the desired effect. But the other woman will require a little more effort, I believe. And you, D! I already have one for you in my possession. We shall soon see exactly how long your dhampir blood can fight my powers of persuasion."

After the sun went down, the roar of the surf suddenly grew much closer. Even at Su-In's home, where the footsteps of those busy preparing for the wake never died down, the sea sounded bleak and forlorn.

D was in the barn. The remains of Su-In's grandfather were being kept out there, coffin and all. There was no shortage of demons looking to invade a body whose soul had departed. To prevent them from doing so, corpses would be washed and purified with salt water, and their veins would be filled with spring water. The only other preparations consisted of having the mortal remains spend the night in the barn, which now had protective wards against demons posted in sixteen different spots. The people who'd found the body had done the salt water purification ceremony, while the doctor had injected the spring water. The head monk from the local temple would've ordinarily traced a circle around the barn to keep evil spirits at bay, but he wasn't around at the moment as he'd been called away by a major disaster in a nearby fishing village. Fortunately, a traveling holy man who was staying at the village inn was convinced to do the final part. The reason D was now stationed there was because, even after every possible precaution had been taken, there were still some entities that needed only the tiniest opening to slip into someone else's flesh.

Su-In was in the main house, busy with preparations for the wake. Visitors would be coming by to pay their respects to the deceased after midnight. It was 9:00 Night now.

The footsteps that sounded outside the barn had reached D's ears from a long way off. Shortly thereafter, there was a knock at the sliding door and one of the neighborhood women who was helping out poked her head in. Flushing crimson, she told the Hunter he had a visitor. "He's fiftyish and has a bushy beard. He's toting around an iron staff. Says he's got something to tell you."

"Get someone to take my place here."

With these words, D left the barn.

The night was staggeringly dark. There was no moon or stars— only the voice of the tides could be heard, singing about the sea.

Not entering the main house, the Hunter instead circled around to the front door.

A bored-looking man stood under the eaves. He looked more like a messenger who'd come to deliver some news than someone who'd come to pick a fight. Not only was there no lust for killing about him, but the way his towering frame was stooped over and peering in through one of the windows was almost comical.

"You have business with me?" D called out from beside him.

Turning around in surprise, the man had a sparkle in his eyes. The light by the front door painted gleaming highlights on the bushy black growth that covered his face from the nose down.

Suddenly drawing himself up, the giant of a man said in an unexpectedly dignified tone, "Nice to meet you. I'm 'King Egbert.' I'm one of the five that find themselves in Gilligan's service. At the moment, I'm working on my own. Two of the others have already had the pleasure of meeting you, haven't they?"

Here the man held his tongue to see D's reaction, but the utter lack of response left him off-balance. Coughing, he added, "I'm not real big on subterfuge, you know. If we're to fight, I want to do it fair and square. Though if you were to just give me the bead, we could end this without even doing that."

"Where should we do this?"

The curt and cold nature of D's reply left Egbert flabbergasted. "You mean to tell me we can't talk this over?" he asked as he stroked his impressive beard.

"If it's the bead you're after, we won't give it to you."

"Hmm. Then I guess you're going to force my hand. That's a pity."

The real question was why the man had said it was a pity. Could he sense D's true power, or was he referring instead to the good looks the Hunter stood to lose?

Shifting the seven-foot-long iron staff he had under his left arm to his right hand instead, the man said, "Well, would you step over there with me? After all, I don't want to spoil the funeral by getting blood all over the place."

"It was one of your friends who killed him," D said icily.

Indignantly Egbert shot back, "You'd better watch your mouth. I don't rely on anyone but myself. There's nothing I loathe more than taking on co-conspirators. What he did has nothing to do with me."

"Maybe in theory."

"At any rate, we can do it over here," the bearded man said as he left the property first and walked toward the seashore.

Crossing the street, he leapt off a stone embankment and landed on the sand ten feet below. The flashy way he landed, kicking sand up everywhere and looking like he was going to lose his balance, might've been a trick to lull his opponent into complacency. If it wasn't, it didn't seemly likely he would've been fit to work as a warrior or bodyguard.

Seeing D touch down softly, he groaned appreciatively, "You certainly are something, aren't you? I could've extended my country from here all the way up to that house, but I figure there's no need to show off."

Walking another hundred feet toward where the surf lapped at the shore, Egbert then halted—only the waves made any appreciable sound. The water's edge was less than thirty feet away. The darkness was like a heavy coat of lacquer, yet through that murk, D's eyes could discern the enormous ring that encircled both Egbert and himself. Further scrutiny would reveal that strange bumps and hollows dotted its interior. These shapes were bits of tree branches artlessly stuck in the soft sand, rocks that'd been set there, and a long, thin ditch that looked to have been scooped out by someone's fingers.

"Think this is strange?" Egbert asked as he rested the iron staff against his shoulder. Although his tone was solemn, the gap between that and his easy manner would've been enough to make the average person tilt his or her head in puzzlement. "This is my kingdom. All of it is mine to command. I could make it larger if I liked, but it'd take some time to bring it under my control. Well, I suppose this is a reasonable size. But before we do anything—" Egbert began as if something had just occurred to him, then he took a dozen steps that brought him outside the closest edge of the ring. "Come with me. Let's try this outside my country."

D stepped out of the circle, too.

Upon leaving about ten feet between them, the opponents squared off.

Letting out a breath, Egbert locked the iron staff under his arm. He never dropped his guard for a second. As warriors went, he was first-rate.

First-rate—the term had a hollow ring to it when you were face-to-face with D.

A blur of black as he went for the sheath on his back, D drew his weapon, too. The tip of his sword was low, stopping just shy of touching the sand. Though it was almost impossible for most swordsmen to bisect their opponent when bringing the blade up from such a low position, it was even more difficult for a foe to parry it.

"So after I win I guess I get the bead, but where should I look for it?"

D replied to this impudent remark by extending his left hand. His fist opened.

Seeing what lay in it, Egbert nodded. "Okay—let's do this!"

The sand that covered one of Egbert's feet started to rise. Feinting a charge, he stopped cold as a stone statue.

D had become darkness itself, and an unearthly aura gusted from the tip of his blade.

The man's innards chilled, his muscles and nerves shrank back.

"Vampire Hunter D . . ." Egbert said, his frozen tongue moving as if in a dream. "I finally realize the full weight that name carries. I don't care how tough a Noble might be . . . it wouldn't mean squat up against you . . ." Just as his hoarse groan dwindled, his iron staff lashed out.

Though he hadn't seen D move, the instant Egbert felt his blow parried, he made a horizontal sweep with his staff. There was a sound of otherworldly beauty, and sparks shot out. Knowing simply from the vibrations transmitted to the palm of his clenched hand that the tip of his staff had been severed, he truly was a first-rate combatant.

A flash of black mowed without hesitation through Egbert's neck. Or more precisely, where his neck *had been*. Coincidences like this were one in a million. Egbert had avoided D's deadly slash by falling flat on the ground. Although totally involuntary, the move had saved him by a hairsbreadth. But as proof that he was indeed a warrior, Egbert hurled the staff he held at D before the Hunter could bring another blow down on him, then threw himself into the circle.

D wasn't the sort to just let a fleeing foe escape. Easily dodging the iron staff, he entered the circle at the very moment Egbert got to his feet. Once more the Hunter's blade sped toward his opponent's torso. Something flashed up into D's field of view, and then there was the *thunk!* of his blade hacking into something hard. A few seconds later, it fell over, raining leaves and branches on the ground. It was a tree trunk, seven feet tall and eight inches thick. It had delayed D's blade a second and saved Egbert's life. And it had suddenly appeared where there'd been nothing before. But no, D alone saw that wasn't entirely the case—he'd clearly seen it growing up out of the ground. Growing from a little piece of branch.

As D tried to pursue the fleeing Egbert, three trees sprang up in rapid succession, clustered tightly together right in front of the Hunter. Slashing right through them, D slipped between the trunks of what were clearly genuine trees before they'd even fallen over. He was greeted by Egbert, who stood ready with another iron staff he'd obviously kept buried in the sand.

II

D's eyes were infused with an eerie light—he'd just realized the unbelievable changes that had come over both Egbert and himself.

Egbert seemed swollen to twice his normal size—not in corporeal terms, but so far as the confidence and power his physique exuded. As if to prove that was no trick of the mind, he cried, "Take that!" and made a thrust with his staff that was ten times faster than before.

Although D did an excellent job of parrying the blow, he reeled from it, knocked off-balance. His sword was heavy. So was his body. It was so strange, as if his flesh had suddenly turned to lead, or gravity itself had been changed.

"How do you like that, Vampire Hunter?" Egbert said, his tone just as dignified as before. But as he held the staff rock steady, the intensity of the killing lust that radiated from the end of it was beyond comparison to when he'd first challenged D.

Without warning, the end of the staff vanished. Feeling the force of the wind as the weapon shot up from below toward his left temple, D didn't back away, but moved forward instead.

Contact! There was the crack of what could only be a bone snapping. But that sound was joined by a cry of astonishment.

If nothing else, the act had been reckless. D's left wrist had stopped the iron staff as it ripped through the air, and through the opening left by Egbert's surprise the Hunter had stabbed the other man in the left side of his chest. The giant reeled back without a word, bright blood gushing from him as the sword came out.

Upon realizing that the thrust that should've gone through his foe's heart had missed the vital point, D was about to advance when suddenly the ground at his feet gave way. A second later his body was knee-deep in the sand, but only for an instant before the hem of his coat spread like wings and he took to the air.

Following after him like some bizarre hand was a long streamer from his knees down to his ankles. Falling to the ground, it sent up a splash. The ground had turned to water, and the thing wrapped around D's leg had been a watery tendril, too.

Sand bouncing up sharply around his feet as he landed, D leapt once more and came back to earth on ordinary ground.

"I thought you'd fall in, but you're even better than I expected," Egbert could be heard to say from some forty feet away, and it was obvious from the sound of his voice he was choking back his pain. "But do you think you can reach me here?"

D didn't answer, and he didn't move.

Waves were breaking at his feet. The shoreline was over thirty feet away—yet still there were waves here. And who else but D would've noticed that tiny ripples were spreading out from Egbert's feet in all directions? Had there been any moonlight, the small but unmistakable crests on them would've glittered visibly. The sands were becoming a sea. A sea forty feet wide, all inside the circle Egbert had scribed.

"Can you reach me?" Egbert asked in a low voice. "Gravity, the woods, and now the sea itself all protect me. And that's not all. Here's something else—you have to see this," he laughed. "The soldiers of my kingdom!"

Something else came into being in the breaking waves. First, black spheres came to the surface. Heads. Their nature was made apparent by the shoulders, arms, and torsos below them as they rose smoothly. Perhaps it was because these "fake" beings had just risen from the sea, but water dripped lazily from the seaweed-like hair that fell over their foreheads, and it wouldn't have been at all surprising if their eyes had glazed over and fallen right out. From the neck down they were like the soldiers one might see in a hologram collection for children in the traveling library, dressed in primitive armor and armed with crude swords. Completely filling D's field of view, there were more than a dozen of them.

Coughing and clearing their throats, they spit out blackish wads. Spattering against the waves, these turned out to be sand. They then turned their black faces to the heavens, and the silence was broken by the sound of them inhaling one after another. Spitting out the sand that clogged their windpipes and drawing in the fresh air, these "soldiers" were imbued with "life."

"I can make mountains, if need be. Or rivers, or even vampires," Egbert said, his voice inebriated with self-love even as he pressed down on the shoulder wound that wouldn't stop bleeding. But he could probably do exactly what he said. Inside the ring he'd scribed in the sand—this eldritch zone he'd established—he was the absolute ruler, a monarch without peer. With but a single command from him a stick would become a stand of trees, a puddle became the sea, and mud figurines he'd prepared were transformed into the mightiest of soldiers. Here in his self-made "kingdom."

The metallic scabbards rasped as the soldiers drew their swords.

D didn't move. Although the sea didn't look like it'd come up past his ankles, he'd already determined that it was actually incredibly deep. Now a stranger in this land, he had to consider every possible element his enemy.

"His left hand is useless—attack him from that side!" Egbert shouted.

At his command, his soldiers charged at D with their glittering blades.

But they probably never heard a hoarse voice howl, "His left hand is useless, eh? I'll show you!"

Suddenly there was a powerful gust of wind. Waves began to build and break on the sea that lay in defense of Egbert, and in the blink of an eye, the vast body of water became a thin layer of liquid suspended in the air. All the wind was blowing toward a single point. Toward D—and his supposedly broken left hand.

And what a powerful gale it was. But it didn't blow the soldiers through the air. Before it could, the tendrils of wind had already ripped away the flesh and blood that formed their bodies. Necks twisted, arms snapped, and the torsos they'd been joined to broke apart in midair, returning to their original form—sand, to be precise—before they were sucked into D's left hand.

Perhaps it was the combination of this terrible shock and the pain in Egbert's shoulder, but his spell seemed to falter as the soldiers, the protective grove, and the surface of the sea all vanished. Huddled on the beach, Egbert was left as exposed as the fairy-tale emperor in his new clothes.

With his blade in his right hand, D paced forebodingly toward his foe. A contest of this sort always ended in death. That was the iron rule for those who made a business of doing battle.

Egbert looked up. In another second, there'd be a bloody horizontal swipe just below his fearful, upturned face.

But D's blade stopped in midair.

"I'm not going to kill you," the Hunter told him. "I have a message for your friends. Tell them I have the bead. And if they want it, it's *me* they should come after."

The eyes of the two men met, and sparks seemed to fly. And then there was a surprised cry of "Oh!" from somewhere.

D turned toward the sea.

There was no moon. Not even the stars were visible. But D, of all people, could still see. Over by where the stark waves broke, out in the water less than fifteen feet from shore, stood a caped figure submerged up to his waist. The wind that drove the waves also carried an ineffable aura that buffeted D's cheeks.

"Baron Meinster—are you back from the sea?" D said, his words drifting far off into a darkness forsaken by light.

However, their confrontation lasted mere seconds. The sea behind the figure seemed to suddenly build, and a massive wave filled D's field of view. And after that had wiped the surface clean, there was no sign of life whatsoever.

Somewhere, a seagull cried. The surf made the only other sound.

Sheathing his blade, D looked over his shoulder. There was no sign of Egbert. Not even his bloodstains remained. And that was no mean feat.

"Did you see that?" D's left hand asked.

"Yes."

"He was pretty intense. In all my days, I've never heard of such a thing. Wind up on the wrong side of him, and it could spell trouble for you."

"Yes, it might."

"Yeah, but there's something else," the voice said introspectively. "I don't quite know what it is, but he doesn't seem like ordinary Nobility, either. He's a Noble, but then again he's not. Like someone else I know. He had the same feel to him. And another thing . . ."

D turned to look off over the roaring surf., as if something he'd lost lay out there.

The voice said, "He had the saddest eyes. Crazy for blood, but truly sad at the same time. That's just like someone else, too."

D's hair flowed out around him. Apparently the wind had changed direction. The wind coming off the freezing sea was terribly cold.

"The north wind?" said the voice. "The north sea, you, and him. If you were to leave town right now, you might save yourself from something you'll only want to forget."

D didn't reply. A short while later, the gorgeous figure turned his back on the eternal voice of the sea.

When he returned to Su-In's home, he found there'd been some excitement—it seemed someone had broken into one of the back bedrooms and ransacked it. When D stepped into Su-In's room, everything was in such disarray it looked like a miniature hurricane had torn through it.

From what Su-In and the neighborhood women helping her said, around the time D went down to the beach they had finished decorating for the wake and everyone was taking a break in the living room when they distinctly heard the sound of one thing after another hitting the floor. Now, these were housewives, but these women not only lived out on the Frontier, but in a village full of fishermen. Not knowing whether this was a burglar out to capitalize on someone's hour of misfortune or some spirit looking for a body to possess, they took harpoons and machetes in hand and noisily made their way to the back of the house with prayer beads and other talismans held out in front of them. Though burglars and the vast majority of carnivores would've fled at the sound of their footsteps, this thing was completely undeterred, continuing to tear the room apart even as the group pounded away at the door.

Now infuriated, the women wanted to get the door or window open, but that didn't work—they seemed to be locked. When they asked Su-In about it, she said she'd locked up just to be safe. The key was brought quickly and slotted into the keyhole, where it turned easily enough. But the door itself still wouldn't budge at all. Someone suggested they try to get in through the window, but that had been locked from the inside and the glass itself seemed to have a sort of semi-translucent film over it. Perhaps that was why when they hit it with a rock the glass cracked but wouldn't come apart at all.

One short-tempered matron became furious and, shouting that she'd gladly pay to replace the door, hammered away at it with the ax they used to split firewood. Apparently there was none of the weird film there, as the ax sank deep into the door. Even the audacious burglar must've been startled by that, as the racket inside ceased immediately, and then one of the neighborhood women with a hint of extrasensory perception informed them that all signs of anyone being in there had already vanished. As the woman declared, "The culprit's gone," they broke in the door and the whole group charged in, only a minute or so having passed since the first blow of the ax.

It was five minutes later, after an exhaustive search of the ransacked room, that they learned it was just as the housewife had said. The window was locked, too. Before the ruckus, Su-In had secured it just as she'd done with the door. And the culprit hadn't left by either of them. How had he or she even gotten in to begin with? The only direct way outside was the window on the southern side, but not only had it been coated with the same strange mucus—probably to prevent anyone from interfering with his or her work—but it was also still locked. As for the door, it had the same mucus on all four edges, which was why it wouldn't open even after it'd been unlocked.

The mucus—or gelatinous substance—was quite unusual. It was flexible and soft to the touch, like gelatin or a jellyfish, yet once it had been stretched a certain distance it became hard as steel and impossible to cut. Anything set on its surface would stick to it like glue so that no amount of pushing or pulling could budge it.

After the circumstances had been explained and D had inspected the room and the strange substance, he told Su-In, "I know who did this."

Su-In's eyes bulged in their sockets. "But—how in the world could someone manage this?"

"That I don't know," D said nonchalantly.

The reply was a tad dismissive, but when it came from this young man's mouth it somehow seemed like he was imparting some great universal truth, and Su-In couldn't very well complain.

"You don't know how, and yet you still know who's responsible?" she asked.

"This is the same as the skin off that character who impersonated your grandfather this morning. It's in a different state, but the basic substance is one and the same."

"In that case, you think that impostor broke in here to steal the bead?"

"Undoubtedly that was the aim."

Su-In made a dubious expression. The blow that'd cut deep into Twin's shoulder hadn't sprung to mind. After being wounded that badly, not even the toughest person would feel like coming back there the same day to rob the place. "Okay, then who did it, and how'd they get inside?"

"Is there anyone in the barn?" asked D.

"Mr. Kotoff."

Accompanied by Su-In, D left the main house. Perhaps sensing that something was wrong, Su-In sped ahead to the barn and opened the door. The coffin rested on a row of wooden boxes, and before it was a man with graying hair who was snoring to beat the band. A bottle of cheap liquor stood vigilantly beside the box on which the man's head rested. Not surprisingly, only about a third of its contents remained.

D and Su-In made a thorough inspection of the area around the coffin. Nothing was out of place. Even the seal on it to ward off demons was still intact.

"Should we open it?" Su-In asked, looking at D as she reached for the lid of the coffin.

Signaling to the girl to stay back, D opened the lid instead.

Grampa Han lay there in his coffin looking exactly as he had when Sun-In had placed him in it.

"Looks like nothing's out of the ordinary, right?"

"You should get that guy out of here," the Hunter told her. "He's of no use to us like this."

"D . . ." Su-In started to say, fear swimming in her eyes for the first time as she gazed at the Hunter. Quickly nodding her assent, she lifted Kotoff up. Easily shouldering a body that looked to weigh at least a hundred and seventy pounds, the woman walked out without a backward glance.

Once the door had been shut and Su-In's footsteps had faded into the distance, D tugged the wool sweater Grampa Han was wearing up over the old man's chest. Pulling a silver dagger from the inside lining of his coat with his left hand, he drove it into the old man's heart without a second's hesitation. There was no reaction at all from the paraffin-pale body.

Whether or not that result was satisfactory couldn't be discerned from the Hunter's handsome but emotionless face as D pulled the old man's sweater back down and closed the coffin's lid.

"Is that what you were expecting?" D's left hand asked.

"I don't know."

"Burglars these days must be getting pretty clever. At any rate, once they know you're in possession of the thing, nothing too bad should happen. So, what were you planning on doing next?"

"You saw him, too," said D.

"Damn. As if the summer wasn't short enough to begin with, now we've got one problem springing up after another. It's gonna rain blood. That's what your fortune says."

"My fortune?"

"That's right," D's left hand replied. "I recently learned how to tell fortunes from the wind. Depending on the direction, the timbre of it, and whether it's strong or weak, you can tell if good things or bad are coming."

"And where did you learn all this?" D asked, completely unfazed.

"Right here, of course. Smack in the middle of your grubby little mitt."

"When?"

"Little bits here and there, whenever you weren't working me like a dog," the voice replied grumpily. "After a hard day's work, most folks whine about how tired they are and how they just can't wait to get some sleep. But those with willpower show those heavy eyelids who's boss and go right on working. That's the only way wise people come to be in this world. The wind taught me that. And it said that before the summer's over, winds of misery will blow through here colored with vermilion. Any way you look at it, the days are just gonna get harder and harder starting tomorrow."

"You were as powerless as I expected, weren't you?" asked the voice of someone on an elegantly carved sofa in the darkness. The shadowy figure lay at length on the piece of furniture. The voice was that of Shin.

"He's a fearsome character, to be sure," Egbert said with a sigh, not completely admitting defeat. Although there was no hint of pain in his voice, the feeling of exhaustion was undeniable. Whether the compatriots and competitors that surrounded him would believe that was another matter entirely. For these men and this woman, remaining suspicious was the very best way to remain alive. "That's no ordinary Hunter," Egbert continued.

"He's a dhampir," said Twin. His voice came from beside the black door. "And he's not an ordinary dhampir, either."

"You mean to tell me there are different ranks of dhampirs?"

"Damned if I know. At any rate, I'm not sure any one of us could go head-to-head with him and come out on top."

"See, I told you so," Shin said in a reproachful tone. "There's no saying we couldn't take him out one-on-one with proper planning, but even then, there's a strong probability of us being killed. That cold steel and the eerie aura around him—just thinking back on them scares me. I guess the only thing we can do is join forces, right?"

"It's a little early to be doing that," Twin interrupted. "Two of the others haven't come back yet—the mature Ms. Samon and Gyohki."

"How do you know she's mature if you've never seen her face?" Egbert asked, his voice echoing from the center of the room. "I always thought of you as an old shit."

Cackling, Twin replied, "Relax. I wouldn't fiddle around with an old bird like that."

"Just what are you trying to say?!" Egbert shot back.

Following that outburst that hardly suited his solemn tone, the strange zone fell into darkness.

At that moment, someone with an unmistakably voluptuous figure came in.

"Speak of the devil," Shin said with amusement. "So, how did it go? Was it worth it for us to hang around here?"

"I was interrupted," the woman replied in a voice that carried a remarkable weight of scorn—an emotion that was directed at herself.

"You too, huh?"

At Egbert's remark, Samon snapped back, "For your information, it wasn't the man known as D. It was someone else who uses a strange power. I was so close to taking the girl captive and getting the bead. The next time I run into him, I'll tear him to pieces," Samon said, although she hadn't even seen the person using that sorcery—Professor Krolock. All she could recall were the eerie suggestions whispered in her ear. Her display of rage was ninety-nine percent genuine, with the last one percent mere vanity.

"Who was he?"

"I don't know. I didn't see his face."

"So, in other words, he beat you like a dog and you don't even know who he is?"

Samon bit her lip. A thin streak of black ran from that beautiful rose petal. Blood.

"Well, no matter who it was, you blew it, too," Shin said in a tone that seemed intended to cow all the others.

"I wouldn't be so quick to say that," she replied.

"Okay, whatever you say. But it's clear a new opponent has arrived on the scene. If we all go off doing our own thing without knowing who that is, we'll be leaving ourselves wide open. We may not know who he is, but he probably knows about us. You should be reproaching yourself instead of overestimating your own abilities."

"What about Gyohki?" Twin said in a snickering voice that seemed to hang in the air like a balloon.

"He always wants everything for himself. Don't think there'd be much point in asking him," said Egbert.

"Then what do you say we leave him out of our alliance?"

"That'll be great," Twin could be heard to say as he clapped his hands with childlike glee.

"How about you, Samon?" asked Shin.

"Do whatever you like," she said, assenting with surprising ease.

"Then it's decided. Okay, I'll take charge."

For an instant, a rebellious feeling churned through the murky chamber, but the reason it settled again so quickly might've been respect for the speaker's age, or that all of them understood this arrangement was only for the time being.

"So, what'll we do?" Egbert asked.

"Before we get down to that, I've got a few questions. For you in particular, Samon."

"And what would they be?"

"You told us someone put a spell on you, but how did you get free of it?"

The answer wasn't soon in coming.

After a span of five or six breaths, she replied, "I was free of it before I knew it."

"Hmm. And you, Twin—you've been acting kind of odd," said Shin. "You're strangely cheerful. What are you hiding from us?"

There was a burst of laughter flavored with the aforementioned cheer. Though his silhouette was barely visible, his left shoulder looked bigger, no doubt being heavily wrapped in bandages. Yet for all that he was remarkably upbeat. "Stop jumping into this boss thing and being so suspicious of everyone. Don't bring stuff up until you've got something to go on. Okay? Not till you've got something."

"Everyone's a critic," Shin said in return, though his tone was not one of anger or disgust, but rather one of sheer delight. "Fine. We've all got our own little secret schemes. If we didn't, we wouldn't be working together on this in the first place. Okay, listen up. This is my plan."

There in the darkness, the murk then seemed to take on a new and heavier layer.

III

The next morning, D left the barn and walked down to the beach. It was early morning, and while there was a melted sort of light out, some of the darkness of night yet remained. Ash-gray clouds hung in the sky. Down on the beach, where the surf beat against the sand, there was a row of powerboats some fifteen to twenty feet from the edge of where Egbert's "kingdom" had hosted a deadly battle the previous night. Each of them rested on wooden rails—an arrangement that made it possible to push them down to the sea without too much exertion. The boats themselves were roughly fifteen feet long and seven feet across at the widest point. When packed with two or three tons of cargo, that barely left room for a lone helmsman.

He saw Su-In up mopping the deck of a boat. She wore rubber gloves. A rubber apron covered the front of her, and while the Hunter couldn't see her feet, she probably had rubber boots on as well. Sweat beaded on her sunburnt skin. The morning was so still, the sound of her mop on the boards and her breathing seemed louder than the waves. The breath that spilled from Su-In's lips was a mass of white that scattered like a fog. Behind her loomed the rugged cliffs, dark and twisted.

Stretching her back, Su-In put a hand on her hip before she turned in D's direction and gave a small cry of surprise. "You're up early. You should still be sleeping. Oh, I forgot daytime is when you—" she started to say, and then hurriedly covered her mouth with one hand. Her eyes were filled with uncertainty as she watched for D's reaction, but she soon grinned again. The dhampir didn't seem to mind a bit.

"The funeral is in four hours," D said from the beach below.

Grampa Han's remains were going to be interred in the backyard. The Hunter seemed to be implying she might want to take it easy.

"I won't accomplish much moping around and thinking about the deceased, you know. I've got to concentrate on what I'm gonna do from here on out instead. Once we've buried my grandfather, I'm heading out to go fishing."

As the woman wiped the sweat from her brow, D watched her silently. "If you've finished cleaning that up, I'd like to ask you about something," he finally said.

"Sure thing. Don't be shy—ask away."

"Is Meinster's castle very far from here?"

"Yeah. If you're going overland, it's about an hour on horseback from that fork in the road."

"And by boat?"

Somewhat aghast, Su-In replied, "It's less than thirty minutes if you go along the shore. Why do you ask?"

"There's something I'd like to see."

Su-In's lip stuck out as she reflected on that remark, but then she suddenly took her plump hands and smacked her even plumper cheeks before replying, "Okay. I'll take you. On the water or even in it, I'll be just as safe so long as you're with me."

After they'd gone ten minutes, the beach vanished and sheer cliffs that had to be two hundred to two hundred and fifty feet high could be seen off the boat's starboard side as they left waves in their wake. The black cliffs were like a solid wall, with almost no crags or crevasses of any kind. There wasn't a hint of green on them, either.

"It's like this all the way to where the Nobility had their cottages. I'm sure they must've made it that way. One theory is they did it so the creatures they made out at sea couldn't come back to them,"

Su-In explained from the tiny pilothouse, which was shielded by fiberglass on three sides.

There was almost no swell on the sea. Though it felt like there was a breeze blowing out of the west, it apparently wasn't strong enough to whip up any crests.

"Take a look down below," she said to the gorgeous figure standing at the prow.

D turned his gaze from the cliffs. In the dark waters below them, foot-long black shapes swam past elegantly.

"There's a treasure trove of fish in this area. Especially in our one week of summer, when the currents change and push in more kinds of fish than I can count. Although there are some nasty varieties in there, too. What's wrong?" Su-In suddenly asked, having sensed something from D's profile. Her heartbeat was racing.

D kept gazing down at the water without replying, but shortly thereafter he looked up and told her it was nothing.

"Well, that's a relief. See, from time to time some strange critters come up from the depths of the sea. If we were to run into something like that, it'd trash a boat this size in nothing flat. That reminds me—can dhampirs swim?"

"What do you think?"

"I don't know. From what I've heard, the thicker the Noble blood in you, the more likely you are to sink like a stone. But somehow I get the feeling you're an exception to the rule."

Fighting the wind, Su-In smoothed her hair back down.

Another twenty minutes passed. Beyond the ever-present cliffs, the outline of the strange land shrouded in a thin fog was becoming clearer and clearer. The first thing to come into view looked to be an endless expanse of smooth green slope beneath the white veil. Closing the distance further, it became clear when the sea breeze stayed out of their eyes that the green was in fact a thick growth of trees, while the white shapes dotted between them appeared to be buildings of some sort.

Columns carved with an incredible level of detail, stylish bay windows with frosted glass that made everything inside look like it was veiled in white silk—around houses whose designs combined the classical with the ultra-modern, a white stairway zipped as if tracing the path of a shooting star. In part of what was barely recognizable as a garden, the orderly rows of high bushes and the tasteful little arbors and lights still remained, though all had long since ceased to have any purpose and it would be clear to any eye that they drowsed now in the light of destruction.

Even knowing that these were ruins left by creatures that'd dwelt in blood-stained darkness, the things to be seen here brought a desolate wind blowing through the viewer's heart. And realizing that she was listening to the song the wind had to sing of the glory of ancient days and of destruction with a boundless sympathy, the woman was shocked.

"The resort area is about four hundred acres, all told. Some scientist that came out from the Capital said roughly ten thousand Nobles used to live there," Su-In said as she guided her boat toward the vast pier. The foggy vista increased. "That's why you see all of these boats here."

D's field of view was filled by a desolate scene. Like the fingers of a corpse reaching from a foggy swamp, prows, masts, and solar panels jutted from the sea, while countless other boats lay on their sides alongside the rusty red hulls of ships. Out in the fleet of orderly moored boats, schooners, and submarines, the only thing that moved were the sea birds that nested on them, and the sole sound that rang out was the pounding of the waves. Skillfully working the engine, Su-In angled her power boat between a white sailing vessel and another boat.

When they were within twenty feet of shore, D turned around. Despite herself, Su-In looked back, too. There was nothing there. The only thing that disturbed the foggy surface of the sea was the white trail flowing along behind their boat. Suddenly remembering what she was doing, Su-In faced forward again.

There was a noise from the water behind them—the sound of bubbles popping.

She didn't turn around. D was staring at her. Fear paralyzed Su-In. She was scared. Terribly scared. Su-In realized she had a beautiful Grim Reaper on board.

But the ominous mood suddenly dissipated. At that very same moment, Su-In stopped the boat. The harbor lay directly ahead of them. The next thing the woman knew, she was soaked with sweat. And she was cold. The chill wasn't in the air, but was a cooling of the very fount of life in her by a primeval frost. Was this the sort of thing those of Noble blood could do?

"What is it?" Su-In asked, trying to keep the fright from showing in her voice. "Is there something in the water?"

"It'd be best to take the overland route back," the Hunter replied.

"I can't do that. I need this boat. My livelihood depends on her."

"I'll bring it back for you."

"You think I'd trust her to an amateur? Don't talk nonsense. You saw something after all, didn't you?"

D said nothing.

Realizing that he was the sort of man who never said anything unless he was absolutely certain about it, Su-In let the matter drop. The soles of her feet were itching.

First D climbed up on the pier, and then he took the mooring line from Su-In and tied it to a pole. "Are we close to Meinster's castle?" he asked.

"We're about a thirty-minute walk away. Even though his is the only castle facing the sea, you can't tie a boat up there."

"Where is it?"

"Over there," Su-In said, pointing toward the slope lined with vacation homes. As she did so, she also slung the belt with the seven-shot spear gun she'd brought from the boat over one shoulder.

Wide stone steps climbed the slope.

"Have you ever been there before?" D asked. The pendant on his chest was giving off a blue glow.

"Yeah, a couple of times when I was a kid."

"Got a lot of gumption," said a ridiculously hoarse voice that was nothing like D's, causing Su-In to stare in disbelief in the direction the words had come from.

"Shall we go?" D said, stepping forward with his left hand balled tightly. On closer inspection, a faint shadow of a smile might've been glimpsed on the Hunter's lips, although he wasn't even aware of it himself.

The pair began to climb the stone steps. Just fifty yards in from the edge of the harbor, the slope had already begun. The staircase wasn't the only thing that traversed the crazy tangle of trees—there were a number of roads running to and fro through them, and a cable car could be seen stopped halfway up the slope. The latter had run not only up and down, but had also gone from side to side as it carried the residents of these lodges down to the wharf or whisked them to dance parties. Somewhat resembling an airship, the elegant body of the cable car was now tangled with green ivy and covered with fallen leaves, buried in the flow of the dawn.

But how many dozens of steps were there?

Tilting her head to one side, Su-In remarked, "You know, this staircase is kind of funny. No matter how many steps you climb, you never get tired."

"That's because the gravity control unit's still functioning."

"Since over a thousand years ago?" she said, only realizing after voicing the question that if this young man said so, it must be true. "The Nobility sure did some incredible things," Su-In exclaimed with wonder. "From time to time, I just don't know what to think. Every time I come around here, the same thought occurs to me. The people who had this awesome civilization beyond our imagining couldn't have drunk the blood of other people and made them their slaves. Now, I know it's not right, but sometimes I think it all must've been a mistake—that maybe one day we're meant to surpass everything that they achieved. And that humans and Nobles are basically the same creature with just small differences, and though one of them advanced a little earlier than the other, someday the other will probably rise to the very same heights, to stand as their equal. D, we're gonna get there too someday, won't we? I know it probably won't be in my lifetime, but maybe in that of my grandchildren or my great-grandchildren . . ."

Su-In looked at D's profile. She got the impression that something which defied the imagination—at least where this young man was concerned—had just skimmed across his beautiful lips. "Hey," she called out to him despite herself.

D turned in her direction. Wearing the same expression he always did.

Su-In found herself with nothing more to say.

D quickly started walking again.

But in her heart, Su-In murmured the words she hadn't been able to speak. *D, did you smile just now?*

"Su-In," D called out to her.

Her heart skipped a beat. It wasn't that she was afraid he'd heard the secret question in her heart. Rather, it was because she realized this was the very first time he'd addressed her by her first name. And she had the feeling that without even being aware of it, she had long since given up all hope of ever hearing him say it.

"Yes?" she shouted back, although what made her do that was a mystery.

"Get behind that tree over on the right. Hurry."

Driven by his soft voice, Su-In ran off and concealed herself behind the massive bole as directed. Twice as big around as a man could reach, the trunk looked like it could withstand even the claws of a giant dragon.

What was happening? For all her fear, Su-In also felt curiosity and a lust for battle stirring within her. She wasn't the sort of woman who'd sit around at home expecting her husband to keep her fat and happy. Raising the spear gun, she flicked off the spring-powered safety with an experienced hand.

Though the fog had already begun to clear, in the lower portion of the stone steps alone it seemed to have become thicker than ever, and though the shapes of the wrecked vessels were dimly visible, the sea itself was lost. A mechanical clanking echoed out of the depths of the whiteness. Something was climbing the stone stairs.

In an instant, the woman realized what it was. *It's that thing from the sea. But what are those footsteps?* Slowly Su-In drew a breath.

A hazy black tinged the fog, and when it took a certain shape, D drew his longsword.

As if it realized that, the thing's footsteps ceased.

Several seconds passed.

"Come on," D said in the direction of the fog.

As if in response to him, the silhouette moved, and the fog gave birth to a bizarre creature.

The Sea in the Ruins

CHAPTER 6

I

I t was reminiscent of a crab made of metal—a crab with ten legs and a carapace ten feet wide. Instead of pincers at the end of those legs, it had scythe-like blades and hooked claws. An opaque glass dome bulged from the center of its exterior, and it seemed to be where the operator would sit. Water dripped from its black metallic body, leaving the stairs behind it wet and glistening. Its gill-like openings seemed to be drainage holes, and every time the pair on either side opened and closed, the collected water splashed down against the marble.

When it halted about fifteen feet from him, D asked tersely, "Who are you?"

There was the sound of meshing gears and something rotating. A black leg rose swiftly. It was at least seven feet long, but because the creature kept them curled under itself like a true crab, the height to the top of its dome was a little less than seven feet. Including the end attachments, each leg had four segments.

A streak of black lightning raced through the air. The leg that'd hooked up at D from below ended in a scythe-like blade. D sprang backward, avoiding it. The black leg stretched. As the tip of the scythe appeared to catch D in the abdomen, Su-In gasped.

There was a beautiful *ching!* and then the scythe went sailing into the air. After D had landed, the savage implement fell on the stairs behind him, sticking into them point-first.

D ran.

There was a hook at the end of the second leg; it curved through the air for D's right side. Dashing along, D pulled his head alone back to let the weapon pass. With a mechanical clicking of joints, the hook stabbed into D's face from the opposite side. But it didn't meet any resistance—D was ducked over. What it'd pierced had merely been an afterimage of him.

The figure in black sprang, gliding like a swallow in flight. As he passed over the giant crab's head, white flashes of light seared through the air. Needles of rough wood ricocheted from the surface of the glass dome.

As D landed several steps below his foe, his coat tore open without a sound. And not just in one place. The collar, the shoulders, and the back were all rent with long thin slashes shaped like bamboo leaves.

Something sliced through the air, then returned to the open launchers on the carapace of the giant crab. It was only a second later that the gnarled tree trunks to either side of D toppled to a roar of rustling foliage. The stumps were cut so smoothly it seemed like it must've been the work of some enchanted blade. Another bole not far off was split halfway through, and from the slice in it something like a thin black string dangled limply. That was the one D had parried with his sword in midair just a split second before landing.

Clearly a complex machine, this giant crab had used powerful compressed gas launchers to unleash dozens of metallic lines at the same time. Roughly three feet long, they had flexible blades so thin they were almost undetectable to the naked eye.

How many people could have avoided dozens of little whips shooting at them at almost four hundred miles per hour—or half the speed of sound? The fact that D hadn't been mortally wounded

was entirely to the credit of his exquisite skill with a sword. However, the foreboding red flowers blooming in confusion at the Hunter's feet were drops of blood. The flesh was rent in a dozen places on his body. Could he weather a second assault? A single vivid streak of vermilion slid down from his right temple, following the line of his cheek.

Compressors whined within the giant crab's launchers, and steam billowed from vents on either side of the creature. It came at him again. But suddenly, the giant crab grew scared.

Although it was a machine and it didn't move an inch, Su-In could tell from behind the big tree that it was frightened. Every fiber of the woman's being was eerily chilled, and her eyes were drawn to D. What had struck fear into the soulless machine emanated from every inch of him. The trickle of blood from his forehead vanished at the edge of his lips. His eyes were ablaze, burning with the color of a vampire's gaze.

The next sight left Su-In wondering if this was the work of a dream demon running amuck in a world where time had stopped.

D kicked off the stone steps. Unlike his earlier leap, this time the hem of his coat opened like the ominous wings of some mystic bird as he soared through the air, and Su-In thought she must be hallucinating. As the shadowy figure came down again, there was a flash of white light from him on the way. Soft as the flash was, it had an incredible weight to it, and even after it had sliced deep into the dome on the giant crab's carapace, the enemy's weapons still didn't go into action. The slice went halfway through the shell. Sparks shot out through the gaping wound, and the giant crab disgorged blood that looked like glistening oil.

Three hooks launched a jerky attack on D, but in a heartbeat they were severed at the second joint and clattered against the marble. D pulled his sword to the right.

With the whir of a motor, the giant crab spun itself about. A crack shot around its center, and while the lower half stayed as it was, the top half rotated ninety degrees. That was where the steel wire launchers were located. There was the sound of a discharge, and the black lines shot off into the treetops.

D made a thrust—a thrust of ungodly speed. It met only empty space.

The hulking form of the giant crab had taken to the air with a gust of wind—and it was flying off into a grove, this thanks to the wires it'd wrapped around the distant trees. Branches snapped and were pushed aside, and as they swung back into place to conceal the black saucer, the sound of trees being torn apart could be heard in the distance. And then there was silence.

Su-In remained behind the tree. "D . . . ," the woman said with concern, though her voice was hoarse. The name came from her unconsciously, and she didn't even hear herself saying it. She was looking at his eyes. That crimson gaze. The pair of fangs that poked from his lips. Here was a Noble the likes of which she'd never seen before. She was scared. He was positively terrifying. Yet this same person was now drenched in blood from his battle to protect her.

Concerns for his safety and another emotion finally overcame the woman's otherworldly horror. Su-In came out from behind the tree. At the same time, D gave his longsword a single shake and returned it to the sheath on his back. Black oil dotted the pathway.

"D . . . ," she said to him, and as she did, D wiped his mouth with his hand. Terror lanced through Su-In once again and she was paralyzed, standing there with one foot on the stone steps.

"Just a moment," D said in a tone that sounded like he was struggling with agony. But it wasn't the pain of his wounds. Gradually, bit by bit, the blood light was fading from his eyes. In the time it took Su-In to blink, his fangs had vanished.

Realizing that the atmosphere around her was pure once again, Su-In let the tension ease from her body. Somehow she managed to walk over to him. "D . . . ," she said, "you're hurt bad . . . But you were incredible. I—I couldn't move a muscle," she stammered.

"The bleeding will stop soon enough," D said impassively.

"What was that thing?"

"I don't know. It could be one of the five sent here, or it could be something else. I've fought three of them, and you met a woman who'd be the fourth. All of them were alive. But that one was dead."

"You mean the machine?"

"There was someone inside," D said, eyeing the grove where the giant crab had disappeared. "Someone who was neither dead nor alive, to be precise."

"Well then—was it a Noble?"

"No, it wasn't like them. It wasn't a dhampir, either."

"I just don't know anymore."

"I'm sure we'll probably see it again," D remarked, turning his gaze back to the top of the staircase. As if to say that was all he'd been interested in from the very beginning. "Let's go."

The two of them started off again. As they climbed the slope, they saw gardens that were frozen in time. In Su-In's eyes, the yellowed grass was lush and green, and her ears echoed with the sound of elegant horse-drawn carriages rolling across the marble roads. It was dusk on a perfectly clear day. A trace of blue yet remained in the ink-black sky, and the breeze that blew through the gardens carried tidings of summer life. Like blossoms, women in white dresses snuggled beside men in black capes, and together they walked the stone paths without shadows at their feet.

Closing her eyes, Su-In could smell the perfume of the night-blooming flowers. On the white terrace of an equally white lodge, a songstress with lengthy tresses sang "The Days You Were Gone" to the accompaniment of a piano. In lighted halls silhouettes danced with gentle steps, while those who'd tired of waltzing stepped out onto the terrace to discuss things in the language of the night, knowing nothing of what was spoken during the day.

At one point Su-In noticed that she'd been crying without even knowing it. A hand came to rest gently on her shoulder. Su-In shook her head from side to side. Though she wanted to turn around and cling sobbing to the chest of the young man behind her, she got the feeling that she really shouldn't. All she could think about was what'd been lost. Her grandfather, her sister, and the Nobility. She would have to live on all alone while conversing with those who decayed. Tomorrow would be another day in this northern village.

Wiping her tears away after a time, Su-In said, "Let's go."

Reaching Meinster's castle in thirty minutes required taking a somewhat dangerous shortcut. Cutting through a garden where grotesque vines wriggled, then crossing over a river on a bridge on the point of collapse, and now taking a path along the edge of the jagged cliff posed no problem for D, of course. Su-In, on the other hand, was astonished that the worst thing that'd happened to her was she was short of breath. Now their eyes were met by the ruins of a stone castle as different from the elegant homes that surrounded it as the heavens were from the earth, and a good deal more unsettling, too. Seen through the narrow slits carved in the outer walls around the grounds, the calm northern sea looked like it'd grown wild, and the clouds that had merely covered the horizon now eddied around the summit of the shattered watchtower.

Su-In softly pulled the collar of her wool coat closed. "It's so cold," she said. "I've come this way before, and it's always been like this. That's why even us locals don't come out here."

As D trained his gaze on the massive fissure ahead of them, he said, "Wait here."

Su-In was speechless. "I didn't come all the way out here just to play tour guide," she finally shouted. "Given what I know about the person who used to live here and the fact that you've come out here, there's got to be some connection to the bead. I need to know what it is. My sister and grandfather were both killed—I mean, they both *died* because of it."

The woman said nothing more, and D walked away without a word. Su-In went right after him. Slipping through the crack, the two of them halted. Su-In gasped.

Before them lay a tremendous pit. It was as if some colossal landslide had happened right in the middle of the castle, leaving only part of the outer walls standing. Round and covering acres, the maw of the chasm yawned like a black and bottomless abyss. The circumference had to be a few miles. It was immediately apparent that the remaining walls and ceiling maintained a precarious balance. There was a sense of overwhelming destruction, devoid of pity or restraint.

D walked to the brink of the hole, and the hem of his coat danced back up like a butterfly from the wind. Was it blowing straight out of Hell?

"The man in the black cape . . . ," Su-In muttered in a cramped tone. "But who would go to such lengths to utterly destroy a fiend feared even by his fellow Nobility? There's not a single trace of anything left. It's almost as if it couldn't be allowed to remain here."

D said simply, "I hear waves."

Su-In strained her ears, but could hear nothing.

"I'm going down," D said as he surveyed their surroundings. He'd just been checking whether or not there were any foes around.

"How?" Su-In asked him. "It could be thousands of feet deep for all we know."

"The sides aren't cut perfectly smooth," D said as he peered into the pit below.

"You don't seriously mean—you'd climb down bare-handed?"

"Wait here."

Swallowing hard, Su-In donned an expression as grave as anyone on a suicide mission and said, "I'm going."

"If you fall, I won't save you."

"I'll be okay as long as I'm with you," she replied, though the words were delivered in a monotone. "Carry me on your back."

D turned around without a word. More than Su-In's determination, it may have been the thought of strange creatures attacking her if she were left up there alone that motivated him.

Su-In pressed herself against his powerful back. Even through his heavy coat she could feel his muscles of steel. As she wrapped her legs around his waist, she felt a warm ache deep in her loins.

D bent over—he was at the brink. Lightly they took to the air. As the darkness swallowed her head, Su-In shut her eyes. A second later, she got goose bumps. The wind was hitting her forehead—D was making the descent headfirst. While she wanted to ascertain just how he was doing it, Su-In couldn't open her eyes. Even if she had opened them, she probably wouldn't have believed what she saw, and the circumstances were so extraordinary they might've left her senseless.

The pit walls that seemed perfectly smooth at first glance actually had irregularities of a fraction of an inch. The tips of D's long, pale, and even delicate fingers found those crevices, and like a veritable lizard he made his way straight down the rock face. His speed was unbelievable considering that he had about a hundred pounds on his back. Above them—or below them, going by the way their feet were pointed—the hole grew smaller, dwindled to a little white coin, and then could be seen no more. This darkness had to be artificial.

In place of the light was a wind that blew up from below with increased and annoying strength, and Su-In's ears distinctly caught the sound of breaking waves. The crash of them grew closer and closer, and they were going to hit them any minute—and just as Su-In thought that, her body turned over easily, her hands slipped off the Hunter, and her legs went into the cold water ankle-deep. She was about to latch onto D again without a thought, but then the soft ground that supported her feet kept her from sinking any further.

Su-In opened her eyes. While she was terribly afraid, her curiosity was also quite strong. She couldn't see anything. There was only darkness and the waves that lapped at her ankles.

With the sound of a striking match, there was light. D had just lit an illumination cord designed for travelers. A quarter-inch thick and based on a blend of magnesium and carbonized zirconium, the cord would light just from friction and could even be used underwater. And if left out in the sun for an hour, the cord could also provide warmth. It was an absolute necessity for anyone on the road.

And the sights that came into view with that dazzling light made Su-In gasp.

II

Normally inactive even by broad daylight, the main street of the village was now filled with bizarre characters.

With a palette spattered with a dozen colors in his left hand and a brush in his right, the traveling artist rendered scenes of one exotic land after another on an oversized canvas and a portable easel supported by his belt, then tossed the pictures to the children who lined the street.

Turning flips forward and backward, and then leaping seven feet into the air to twist and turn before landing again softly as a bird, the acrobats were greeted with applause from the people.

With a cheap cigar in his mouth, a troubadour in a silk hat and a swallowtail coat played a violin and sang to the echo lizard on his shoulder:

A love decided on a summer's eve is a tragedy,
Like a maiden's blood, swooning at the beauty of a young Noble, pale and gloomy,
Or the serenade of the darkness played on the winds of the sad highlands . . .

Though reciting the same lyrics any street musician would know, he received a shower of coins from every woman from the youngest maids to the old ladies with bent backs.

In addition, there were also vendors of ice cream, snow cones, watermelon, and candy treats, and though they didn't seem very suitable for the village at present, their expressions brimmed with confidence as they pushed their garishly decorated carts.

Each and every one of them was part of the procession of attractions and hucksters here for the season about to begin in this northern village—that short, week-long summer.

Particularly noticeable in the group was the human pump—who spat out not only flames but water, fog, flowery petals in all the colors of the rainbow, and ultimately little moons and planets—and a little child of about five who rode on a motorized float. Covered with a red sheet, the latter transformed in the blink of an eye into a saber-toothed tiger, a Neanderthal, a fire dragon, and then into a seven-foot-long unicorn the sheet couldn't possibly have concealed. Wherever these two acts went, they were surrounded by the local children, so it took them nearly ten minutes to move forward even three feet.

All of them were out to stir up as much excitement as possible for the summer festival that would begin with the start of summer the following day, and their tents would be pitched out by a certain temple near the edge of town. Following after the seemingly endless succession of performers, the people moved on, leaving the street filled with cheers and dust. Beginning early in the morning, the procession would continue all day, a cheery and bustling sight welcome anywhere on the Frontier.

The showy performances and promotions went on for some time, but after they had died down, only one strange figure remained: the white-haired and white-bearded old man wrapped in a scarlet cloak faced a collapsible metal easel, seated on a shabby folding stool as he moved his pen across the canvas. Unlike the performers here for the festival, he seemed to be a traveling painter merely out to earn a living, and the reason the crowd around him didn't disperse even after the gaudy promoters had gone was because it was rare to see such a scholarly tableau in this fishing village, and the pen, canvas, and ink he was using were unlike those any artist who'd ever been here had used in the past.

In place of a brush he used a sharp quill pen, and for a canvas he had some sort of thin hide. Even more surprising was the ink into which he chose to dip his pen. Sticking his pen into a vein in his own left wrist, the old man dabbed it in the blood that poured out before moving it to his canvas. Knitting their brows at first at the sheer weirdness of this, the villagers had only to take one look at the picture he'd apparently been working on for some time when their shock gave way to enchantment. The women in particular stared raptly at that dangerous face.

One cried, "I want it!"

"Let me have that one!" said another.

"How much do you want for it?" asked a third, offering a handful of coins.

The picture was a portrait of a young man—just the face, not a full-length portrait. Yet the women were all clamoring for the same image as if they couldn't wait for him to finish it, their eyes bloodshot and breath snorting out of their noses.

"You fancy this one, do you?" the old man muttered morosely while etching delicate lines onto the hide with precise movements that seemed unimaginable from his rough-looking hands, where muscles and tendons bulged to the surface. "I can't say I'm overly fond of it myself, so take it if you wish. Put the money in that bag there."

Bending toward the leather bag where the clink of coins instantly began, the old man pulled out the wooden box that was next to it, took off the spring lock, and pulled out a bundle of similar canvases.

The women's eyes were alight like those of savage beasts. All of the parchments in the roll had drawings of the same young man's face. Hands reached in wildly, and a brief but bitter struggle ensued. Though there were surely more canvases than spectators, all of the artwork was carted off, and perhaps because of this there was cursing and tugging and women shouting at other women to give them their pictures back as they all dispersed.

Once they were gone, the old artist pulled a new canvas from his box, put it on his easel, and began to move his pen across it. Not merely interested in earning a living, he seemed rather to be a lone artist completely driven by an urge to create.

And while the old man hadn't noticed, off to the east—at the corner of the first side street headed toward Su-In's house—one woman in a shabby coat had been glaring intently in his direction since just before all the excitement began. Hair disheveled and complexion pale, she looked at first like one of the ubiquitous vagabonds when she was in fact none other than the sole feminine accent in the fiendish quintet—the sorceress Samon. Needless to say, the elderly artist her venomous gaze fell upon in a hair-raising distillation of malice and lust for vengeance was Professor Krolock, while the face on his canvas was that of D.

But what in the world could he be doing here? Why was Samon looking at him with such loathing, as if she knew he was the one to settle with when she didn't even know what he looked like? And finally, how had this woman who should've obeyed the professor's whispered commands to kill herself returned to the group unharmed? The answer to that riddle would come soon enough.

Folding up his easel and stool, the professor tossed them back into the same wooden box and exclaimed, "My, now! Only two days ago I was destitute. Well, I've got enough for the inn and some funds to live on now."

Apparently he'd disposed of the pictures to raise some money.

"Which way was it to the inn again?" he said to himself.

As the old man walked off in the opposite direction, Samon turned right around and started following after him with a perfectly innocent look on her face.

In a few minutes, he came to a vacant lot with no sign of anyone else around. Quite a way off, a little stone building that was probably a storehouse stood all alone, and the old man circled around behind it.

A knowing smile rose to Samon's lips. Calmly shutting her eyes, she brought her hands together and interlocked them with only her index fingers extended. A few seconds later, when she came around behind the building, the old artist she pursued was there waiting for her.

Neither of them seemed at all ruffled.

"You knew what I was up to, did you?" Krolock inquired.

"There are no inns out this way," Samon chided him.

"Ah, you have excellent hearing."

"Yes, that's why I heard your voice before. Heard it as you ordered me to my doom."

"You must be a lucky woman," said the old man. "But this is more than I can attribute to poor luck on my part. Perhaps my sketch was a tad too rough? No, I'm sure there must be some other reason."

"That's none of your business. You'll die without ever knowing."

"My name is Professor Krolock. You may take that information to your grave."

"I'm Samon. And you've taken the words right out of my mouth." Samon's lips rose in a malevolent bow. All was in readiness for her spell.

The professor formed a little grin in the middle of his white beard. "What's wrong?" he asked. "Would you prefer that I start first?"

The sorceress' gorgeous mien twisted with distress. In point of fact, her powers should've long since taken effect.

Samon's spell had the power to take the fondest memories a person had and magnify their nostalgic feelings, giving shape to them in a way that would melt a person's willpower to nothing. What doting parent could look on their beloved child, appearing just as he or she had in life, and not heed whatever request the child might lisp? Even if they had enough reason to realize such a thing was impossible, Samon's power would drown their thought processes in the sweet nectar of remembrance, guaranteeing their acquiescence.

But she never would've dreamt there existed anyone whom this power couldn't affect.

"How unfortunate," the professor said as he rubbed at his eyelid with one hand. "You see, I don't carry around that sort of bothersome baggage." With a flourish of his arm, a rolled-up parchment appeared from his sleeve. He opened it.

Samon raised her right hand.

"Stop," the professor commanded, his tone trenchant.

But there was no chance that a woman of fortitude like Samon—a warrior who'd survived countless deadly encounters—would simply surrender. And yet her right hand, which was about to hurl a gleaming black razor disk, stopped in midair, every muscle stiffened.

The professor's command hadn't been directed at Samon—at least, not at the *real live* Samon. The word he'd barked had been directed at the picture on vellum his right hand held open—a precise rendering of Samon's face.

Sometimes he whispered to it almost like a song. Other times he shouted at it as if enraged. When directed to a peerlessly detailed likeness of a person done in his own blood, his suggestions and instructions would hold the living model for his artwork spellbound.

"I don't know how you survived last time, but this time you won't get away. It's a pity one so beautiful has to die so young, but you'll simply have to count yourself unfortunate that I'm too old to succumb to such looks. Okay, now you're going to climb down to the beach . . ."

But just as the professor gave his deadly commands, a silvery flash shot toward his back. Spinning around without a word and backing away a few steps at the white-hot pain of being slashed open with a blade, the professor saw the dashing young man who held a bloody sword. "Why, you're . . ."

The young man stepped forward calmly.

At the same time the spell that held Samon must have broken, because she shook her head repeatedly and turned toward the professor with curses in her eyes.

The professor's assessment of the situation was rapid. Without any parting repartee, he grabbed the wooden box by his side and ran for dear life toward the street. Blood gushed from the gash in his back.

"Die already!" Samon groaned, ready to hurl her razor disk when the point of a silvery blade quickly came to rest against the base of her throat.

"What are you doing?"

"I could ask you the same," the temptress said, the corners of her eyes rising angrily.

Turning an icy gaze to her, the handsome swordsman—Glen—said, "You didn't show up at the time I set. So I went for a stroll and found you in this fine mess. You haven't forgotten the orders I gave you, have you?"

"I didn't take any orders—" Samon spat as she averted her gaze. The muscles in her cheeks were trembling. Twitches brought about by humiliation—and fear.

"Do you defy me? Then allow me to refresh your memory. When you were about to throw yourself from the cliff behind the temple, it was I who saved you. And after that I—"

"Don't speak of that," Samon said, swinging her right hand.

That same wrist was then caught in a viselike grip, and the woman's alluring face twisted in pain. The razor disk fell at her feet.

"It would appear that old geezer is the very same person who would've had you throw your wretched self from that cliff. In which case, I suppose I should let him get away for being the one who helped bring us together. Besides, you've got other work to attend to, wench."

And then Glen pulled the struggling warrior woman close and pressed his lips to hers so tightly it seemed like he'd rip them right off.

III

Of course, the incandescent glow didn't extend far enough to reveal the scenery for miles around them. All Su-In saw were black waves breaking at her feet and something that looked like a beach to her rear. And above that beach loomed part of some colossal mechanism. The entrance to the hole couldn't be seen at all. But what Su-In thought was that perhaps, contrary to legend, Baron Meinster's accursed experimentation had continued down here in the bowels of the earth.

Pipes crisscrossed the ceiling, and there were rows of pistons that called to mind steam-driven machinery, twisted cords, and a series of cracked glass tanks that nonetheless remained brimming with some unknown fluid. Even this brief glimpse at no more than a portion of the research facility easily conveyed something about how vast the place as a whole was and how unsettling its purpose had been.

"This stuff belonged to Meinster, didn't it?"

Not answering Su-In's question, D looked out over the breaking waves. The light couldn't reach the far side. But Su-In realized this young man could see things she or other people would never comprehend.

"We're under the sea," the Hunter told her. "Well over a mile down. I guess you could say we're underground, too."

"But who could've . . . Do you mean to tell me Baron Meinster survived?"

There was no reply.

"Or did someone kill Meinster and make it look like everything had been destroyed, but secretly continued the same experiments here deep underground . . . Someone like . . . the man in the black cape? Who on earth was he, anyway?"

D didn't answer.

Su-In sensed him moving away. For some reason, it seemed like the awesome mystery that hung in this subterranean abyss had congealed into a dark hue that clung to the back of the gorgeous Vampire Hunter.

They took a dozen steps across the sand. Realizing there was no use saying anything more to D, Su-In kept quiet. She was worried about whether or not they could make it back in time for her grandfather's funeral. They still had two hours, but it would all depend on how long it'd take to climb back out of this hole. Su-In suddenly thought how strange it was she could still worry about such mundane matters.

Relying on the tiny circle of illumination, the pair walked through the laboratory. Startling sights drifted into the light, then

faded again. Beastly corpses beyond numbering floated in the tanks. There were severed limbs and trunks that couldn't be easily classified as either human or animal. But strangest of all was the helix model that spiraled up toward the heavens. The pedestal alone was over six hundred feet in diameter. Although the woman asked D what anyone would ever need one so big for, he naturally failed to reply.

When another tank came into range of the light from D's hand, Su-In froze in amazement. Suspended there in the clear liquid were the corpses of what could only be wolves and bears and fire dragons. But what frightened Su-In was the fact that their hands or chest or some other part of their flesh looked like it had to be human.

So, this was the result of Meinster's experiments. Fear and rage filled Su-In's brain with red. "What was Meinster trying to do? Who took over for him? What did they try to create here? What kind of horrible creature?" she asked, her voice trembling.

Just then, there was a sound of something other than waves out in the subterranean sea. Something had splashed in the water. The realization that they were at the bottom of the sea made the blood drain from Su-In's body. Could it be *him*? This was his lair, wasn't it? Not Meinster, but the "Noble from the Sea," whose true identity was a mystery to all.

"Stay here," the Hunter said as he took her hand and put the light in it. The dark figure dwindled in the distance without a sound. Su-In's stout heart tightened with a kind of fear she'd never felt before.

D stopped at the shore. Even his keen eyes that could see as clearly by the light of a single star as at midday could find no end to the waters. It truly was a sea. What's more, there must've been some need for it down here in the bowels of the earth.

Glub . . . Bubbles rose to the surface roughly forty feet away. Something had let its breath out underwater. The ripples became small waves that reached D's feet.

About seven feet ahead of where the bubbles had risen, something black came to the surface. A human head. Was it the same person he'd seen in the sea the night before?

Slowly, it rose from the water. With every move, the dripping water splashed from its chest, its hips, its thighs. Stopping fifteen feet away from D, it was a strapping man who was stark naked. He wasn't the same individual as the other night—that much was immediately evident. He had an elegant look to him, with features reminiscent of the people of the southern sectors and a well-groomed mustache that only strengthened his impact. With the proper wardrobe, he could probably pass for a Noble.

"You must forgive me for my less-than-presentable state," the man said as he slicked back his hair. "This place brings back so many memories; I simply had to go for a swim."

"So, the sea brings back memories," D said softly. It wasn't a question. Nor was it an opinion he was expressing. "All life came from the sea. That's why he needed the sea to be here."

"I suppose that's the case," the man conceded as he took a few steps and collected his clothing from the darkness. As he pulled on a pair of trousers, he said, "I take it you're D."

"That's right."

"So, we meet at last. Allow me to introduce myself. Gyohki is the name. I'm an ally of Shin and Twin, whom you've already faced. I see now why the two of them didn't fare well. You're like Death on two legs."

"You were created here, weren't you?" said the Hunter.

"Precisely." Pulling on a wool shirt, Gyohki wrung the water from his hair with both hands. "You see," he continued, "I'm one of Baron Meinster's precious children . . . although I ultimately ran away."

If this was the case, it meant that this man had lived for more than a thousand years.

Peering fixedly into the darkness, he said, "I take it that's Miss Su-In behind you. I'm touched she'd go to all the trouble of bringing the bead to me."

"I'm holding onto the bead," D said, thrusting out his left hand.

Seeing what rested in the Hunter's palm, Gyohki nodded. "Very well. I won't lay a hand on the young lady."

"I take it you haven't met up with Egbert or the rest, have you?"

"I've been operating independently since yesterday. I'm not in the same hurry the others are, hence the nostalgic dip here in my birthplace. By the way, I don't suppose you'd simply hand over the bead, would you?"

"My employer wouldn't like that."

"Then I suppose this is unavoidable." Stretching his back, Gyohki then rolled his head from shoulder to shoulder. The bones in his neck cracked loudly. "Ah, I'm getting old," he said with a grin that would've left the female of any species in a daze, but regrettably it had no effect on the Hunter. "Well then—shall we do this?" said Gyohki, his tone intense.

The way both legs were naturally in an open stance and both arms extended before him bore a striking resemblance to how Dwight had looked when he'd challenged D, although this foe differed in that his fingers were open instead of clenched.

The whine of a sword leaving its sheath rose from D's back.

"I have just one question," said D.

"And what would that be?"

"Was it Meinster who made you, or was it *him*?"

As Gyohki exhaled sharply, his leg blasted through the air. The speed of his kick was unbelievable.

Shooting up from below, D's blade met only thin air. Well, not exactly—the Hunter's sword was held flat at eye-level, but Gyohki stood on the blade. His weight seemed to have no effect on the weapon at all.

"Well, what are you going to do now?" the grinning Gyohki asked. "Before you can cut me down, you'll have to knock me off of here first. But all I have to do to take your head clean off is give you a swift kick with one leg. No matter how you look at it, the odds are in my favor. Get the bead out. Do that and I'll spare your life, at least. Hell, I'll even bring the little lady back up top."

D said nothing.

"Such stupidity," Gyohki said, and with that his leg vanished. Or rather, it rocketed toward D's temple with such speed that it seemed to disappear.

A scream rang out.

Postscript

The two volumes of *Mysterious Journey to the North Sea* were to be the first multi-volume tale in the Vampire Hunter D series, which has since gone on to include others like *Dark Road* and *Pale Fallen Angels*. Up until that point, each tale had consisted of three hundred and fifty to four hundred hand-written pages, but along those lines I couldn't tackle any really grand stories. There was also a limit to the number of characters I could use. As a result, I was growing increasingly frustrated. Now, even in a ten-page short story, something is either interesting or it's not, and in a massive five-thousand-page tome you won't tell a story that can't be told. Since I'd already undertaken the Herculean task [*laughs*] of writing a three-volume tale for my first adult-oriented novel, I wasn't particularly worried about penning a thousand pages of Vampire Hunter D.

I adhere to the motto that bigger is better [*laughs*], and even when it comes to boasts and fabrications, I like them as large as possible. I tried to repress that propensity while working on this book, but while I was writing this volume, I stopped and said, "Huh?!" at the scene where D descends into the huge pit (which resembles the scene where the Count goes down the wall in *Bram Stoker's Dracula*). What was it, a mile or more across? As I recall, on the way down D looks back and sees that the opening is far off in the distance, and that it's shrunk down to the size of his little finger. However, if the diameter was more than a mile, D would have to climb down a hundred miles before the opening would seem to shrink to that size. Although I noticed this right away, due to my own foolish nature, I usually let consistency fly off into the depths of space once I get a grand vision in my head. That being said, I didn't want to re-work the image into something weaker. But to climb a mile down into a hole and have an opening as wide as it is deep still gaping above you—that's just comical. Honestly, I was really stuck at that point.

Still, there are parts in *Mysterious Journey to the North Sea* that later works couldn't touch on. The section where D and the heroine visit a Noble's manse and reflect on the beauty of that civilization is something I haven't been able to use since, and it's the scene that best illustrates the "elegance and refinement" of the vampires. I hope that will please all you vampire fans out there. *Mysterious Journey to the North Sea* is actually one of the candidates for the next animated feature—as is a remake of the first story—and if they decide to do this story, I truly hope they include that scene. Though to be perfectly honest, I'm not a big fan of anime at all . . .

To be continued next time [*laughs*].

Hideyuki Kikuchi
November 1, 2006
While watching *Ame no Machi*
(the film adaptation of one of my stories)

And now, a preview of the next novel in the
Vampire Hunter D series

VAMPIRE HUNTER D
VOLUME 8
MYSTERIOUS JOURNEY TO THE NORTH SEA
Part Two

Written by
Hideyuki Kikuchi

Illustrations by
Yoshitaka Amano

English translation by
Kevin Leahy

Coming in September 2007
from Dark Horse Books and Digital Manga Publishing

Summer at Last

I

S and shot up, whipped up by something swinging around at an awful speed. Grains of it scattered in all directions like smoke. There were two massive explosions, and then a second later a human form could be seen on the shore where the black waves broke. It was Gyohki. Standing erect only briefly, he then bent his right knee. Just as he was about to hit the sand, he barely managed to catch himself. A streak of white ran right through his thigh—a needle of unfinished wood.

"You're unbelievable . . . ," Gyohki groaned. Dropping his eyes to his gory thigh, he then turned a look of both admiration and hatred toward the beautiful darkness before him. The darkness that harbored D.

D was just getting up, too. His longsword stretched elegantly from his right hand, as he'd just picked it up from where it'd fallen in the sand. It hadn't actually *fallen*—he'd intentionally dropped it. Just before Gyohki's explosive kick, with true split-second timing, he'd let go of his sword. Rather than getting Gyohki to drop off his blade, he'd dropped him along with his longsword. In order for his opponent to execute that lethal kick to its full efficacy, he needed to have perfect speed and power and to be well balanced, and he'd been thrown off more than enough for D to block the kick aimed at his temple with his right elbow. Before Gyohki could connect with a second kick, D timed it so as to catch his foe's leg and jam a rough wooden needle deep into his attacker's thigh with his left hand.

Seeing the gorgeous silhouette leisurely closing in on him, the limping Gyohki leapt back. A second later he was waist-deep in the water.

"'He who fights and runs away . . .' It's a dated adage, but while there's life there's still hope. I believe I'll call it a day," he said in a tone free from regret. Preparing to dive, Gyohki then suddenly turned his eyes to where D stood at the shore. "You wanted to know who made me, didn't you? Baron Meinster gave me life, but I was perfected by *the other one*."

His body sank straight into the water. Soon splashing could be heard far in the distance, but that was the end of it. He must've swum out into the sea at a depth of seven thousand feet.

Perhaps certain that his foe was gone for good, D returned his longsword to its sheath and walked over toward Su-In. The circle of light from the illumination cord made her location clear in this murk—she was a bit further in than where he'd left her. Though he'd told her to stay there, it would've been hard to imagine a courageous character like Su-In just standing there awaiting her fate. Still, it was strange. If she were to go anywhere else, she most certainly should've gone to check on D, on whom her life depended. But she seemed to have done exactly the reverse and gone in the opposite direction.

D's pace quickened.

Su-In was standing in front of a huge tank they hadn't seen before. Unlike the others, this one was filled with a milky fluid, and it had but a single occupant: a young man who was completely naked. Black and blue marks could be seen on the side that faced her. At a glance it was apparent these weren't wounds that'd been intentionally inflicted on him, but rather had come about through some sudden event. The left side of his forehead was smashed open horribly, leaving a gaping wound you could see through if you looked hard enough. It was almost miraculous that his face had been so perfectly preserved, appearing just as youthful now as it had in life. His left shoulder was also twisted into a strange position—probably the result of a broken bone. No doubt these wounds were all the result of a fall from a considerable height. Judging by his face, he was a young villager. But who would've sealed up his remains more than a thousand years ago?

Not seeming to realize that D was watching her, Su-In kept her gaze trained on the pale, hazy figure. Before long, she muttered, "You fell, didn't you." The way she said the words, they seemed to simply spring into being without ever passing through her thought processes. "You fell—fell at the cape . . . stabbed . . . through the chest . . ."

D looked at the young man's chest. There was no wound there.

Su-In had been talking about someone else.

"Let's go home," D told her.

They had more than enough time until her grandfather's funeral. But considering the way they'd come down, the thought of going back up made a casual term like "trip" seem horribly inadequate. Su-In's body trembled. But before she even had time to think about it, her flesh broke free of her will and she leaned back in D's arms.

Quickly taking the illumination cord, D looked at Su-In's blanched countenance, and then shifted his eyes to the contents of the tank. A corpse floating in a milky liquid and a fisherman's daughter—perhaps the young man's cold eyes could see the thread that joined these two very different lives. But that thread was soon frayed by a tiny groan.

Opening her eyes in the Hunter's powerful arms, Su-In realized the situation she was in and hurriedly tried to stand up. The hue in her eyes as she turned them away from D was ultimately conveyed by the pink that tinged her full cheeks.

"Trying to take advantage of me in a place like this—you should be ashamed!" she said, pushing D's hands away with much more force than was necessary. When she got to her feet again, she was already as steady as a rock. "If we're leaving, what are you gonna do about this place?" she asked as she looked around them. "This was Meinster's research lab, right? If you plan on trashing it, I'll help."

"There are probably traps."

"You've got a point there," the woman conceded.

"It's going to take a while to climb back out. Shall we go?"

"Are you sure it'll be okay?" Su-In asked nervously as she looked up into the darkness above.

Twenty minutes later, as the two of them were leaving the ruins of Meinster's castle, Su-In's gaze had become one of admiration as she stared at D.

After another hour, the pair was greeted by an unexpected sight as they returned home: more than twenty children. As was usual on the Frontier, their height and age, hair color and skin color ran the gamut, but when they saw Su-In and raced over to her, all of their faces glowed with the same expectation. Amid the cries of "Su-In! Su-In!" were some of "teacher," and this prompted D to stare at the sunburnt woman.

"Teacher—when is it?"

"When's school starting?"

Seeming perplexed by the youthful cries, Su-In knit her brow. "That's a good question. I'm sorry, but I don't know if I can do it this year."

Disappointment broke over the children like a wave.

"You see, my grandfather just died, and Wu-Lin's not around either," Su-In said, desperately trying to keep the gloom from her voice.

As the children continued to protest, the shouts of a man and woman who were obviously somebody's parents flew from the main house, saying, "Come on, now! What are you doing pestering Su-In at an awful time like this?" and, "We've got a funeral today!"

Before these rebukes, the children scattered like baby spiders.

Turning to face D, Su-In asked, "You think that's funny?" There was a bit of a challenge to her voice. Not receiving an answer, she continued, "During the summer, I run a school when I'm not out fishing. The kids around here want to know anything and everything. After all, at their age they've never seen anything but the gray sea and our week-long summer."

"Where's the schoolhouse?" asked the Hunter.

"Well, up until last year, we just pitched a tent in our backyard. But this year, they're gonna build a proper schoolhouse. As we rode along the coast, you saw the festival tower, right? It's right next to that. Once that's done, we'll be able to have school even in winter, and we've sent to the Capital for a teacher. The carpenters are working overtime to get it ready by the first day of summer. Looks like they're just gonna make it."

"And is the teacher coming?"

Shifting her eyes to the sea, Su-In replied, "Actually, Wu-Lin was supposed to talk to someone in Cronenberg about that."

Off in the distance, they could hear a child shouting, "Teacher!"

Saying that she had to go get ready, Su-In adjusted her grip on the spear gun and walked off toward the house.

After going in first, D watched the people busily scurrying around the house. "Is this everyone?" he asked.

"Yeah."

Ignoring the gazes of admiration and rapture that fell on him, D went back outside. He told Su-In, who stood by the door, "There's no one dangerous in there."

Lowering her voice, his employer said, "Of course not. They're all folks from the neighborhood. I'm begging you, don't start talking flaky."

"The puppets on the ferry could probably just as easily be disguised as your neighbors."

Tensing at D's words, Su-In said, "I know. We can't let our guard down, right?"

"You should help get ready for the funeral."

"I'm gonna do just that. I leave the rest up to you." With a trusting glance to that inhumanly handsome face, Su-In then went inside.

D circled around to the backyard. The grandfather's remains were going to be buried in one corner—Su-In had stated that would've made her grandfather a lot happier than being interred in the communal cemetery.

Out in the gauzy light of day, suddenly a thin melody and voices joined in song were heard from the verandah out back. The children from earlier were all gathered around a boy of about ten, who was playing a wooden flute.

To you, whom summer brought here,
I give a modest token of thanks.
The white flowers that blossom in the ice freeze all who touch them.
Until the waltz of summer ends,
You are one of us.
And when you go we'll pray for you,
O departing light of summer!

D stood in the languid daylight listening to the earnest, if somewhat off-key, voices of the singers. The shadow cast at his feet was beautiful, but fainter than anyone else's. Off in the distance, the crash of waves could be heard.

And just as it had begun, the singing halted without warning. The boy in the center of the group fiddled with the flute, a troubled look on his face. Putting it to his lips, he inflated his cheeks, but to no effect. Apparently either it was clogged or had a leak of some sort. All around him, the other children asked what was wrong and why it wouldn't play. They were all heartbroken—they'd been sincerely interested in singing. If they hadn't, they'd have long since gone and found something else to amuse themselves.

Their flutist looked ready to cry. His eyes scanned the surrounding area in search of help, coming to rest on the handsome figure. There was no telling just how he could've looked to a ten-year-old psyche. Pushing his way through the children packed around him, the boy ran over to D. Stopping three feet shy of the Hunter, he had both fear and expectation on his face as he looked up reverently.

Not saying a word, D looked down at the innocent face of the dark boy who didn't come up too far past his own waist. The young man's body sank slowly. Down to the same height as the boy.

"What's wrong?" the Vampire Hunter asked.

A tiny hand and the wooden flute it held were thrust out before his eyes.

Powerful yet slender fingers closed on the piece of wood as the Hunter took it from the boy. There were three finger holes, but a threadlike crack ran between the last two. Even patching that wouldn't be enough to get back the original tone of the instrument.

Looking around on the ground at his feet, D then quickly pulled a few wooden needles from the inside of his coat—two of them. Though they were less than an eighth of an inch thick, they were over eight inches long. The thumb of the hand that held the needle reached up for the end of it, and a well-shaped nail protruded ever so slightly from the end of the Hunter's finger. That nail moved in a tiny arc, and two inches of the needle fell to the ground, leaving a perfectly round cut on the end.

The boy's eyes went as wide as if he'd just watched a magic trick.

Adjusting his grip on the needle and taking off the opposite end as well, D then took the other needle and placed its point against one of the round cross-sections. Though he didn't seem to put any force behind it, the new needle slipped into the former needle without any resistance.

There were sounds of surprise all around him. At some point, the children from the verandah had crowded around the Hunter and the boy.

As far as the children could see, the two needles were of equal thickness. And yet the one that'd been pierced hadn't split or broken, and the one doing the piercing slid into the other without hesitation and came out the other side. As the tip came out the other end to the exact same length as the part he'd first sliced off, D pulled the two pieces of wood apart. Then he brought his right hand over to the needle he held in his left. The children caught the glint of a long, thin dagger there, which bored three finger holes with the blade in less than two seconds. Each hole was perfectly round.

Blowing into it once to get the sawdust out of it, D then put the flute to his lips. His cheeks indented ever so slightly, and a thin, mellifluous sound coursed from the instrument.

The multitude of tiny faces changed from looks of amazement to smiles.

Handing the new flute to the boy before him without a word, D stood back up. His eyes shifted to the verandah.

A holy man stood there. Ban'gyoh. Beaming all the while, he tapped at his freshly shaven head as he walked over. Clasping both hands behind his back, he said, "I declare, when a priest isn't reading his prayers, he's got nothing but time on his hands. I've been playing with the children since this morning. And what have you been doing? From what I saw earlier from the kitchen window, it seems you and Ms. Su-In came back on a boat, but you should take care. When a man and a woman recklessly let nature take its course, therein lies the way to lust and temptation."

Muttering a religious incantation in a pleasing tone, Ban'gyoh gazed at D reproachfully. But his heavily wrinkled face broke into a smile as he said, "Though from what it's been my pleasure to see, you have some fine points, too. Usually one as handsome as yourself is cold not only to women, but to everyone aside from himself. But though your veins may be ice, the blood flowing through them seems to have become a bit redder. I have a suggestion for you. Now, I don't know if you're a bodyguard or a warrior or what, but why not abandon the way of the sword for good and look after the children here?" The holy man then laughed, "Oh, I'm just joking with you!"

As soon as he finished speaking, a lovely melody arose from around his feet. The boy had just blown into the flute. Though Ban'gyoh listened to it with his eyes shut, he soon gave a pensive nod. "I hate to say it, but the tone isn't very even," the priest mused. "Child, try playing this."

The young boy seemed perplexed by what the holy man then held under his nose. It was another wooden flute with tiny holes. Roughly two inches shorter than the one D had fashioned, it was also ten times as thick.

"No matter how skillfully constructed the flute may be, there are certain limitations in the instrument itself," said Ban'gyoh. "That one's a bit too tough for a child's throat and lungs. Come now, give it a try."

The child was very forthcoming. Pressing D's flute back against the Hunter's chest, he promptly took the new handiwork from Ban'gyoh and brought it to his mouth. The sound that filled the air was deeper and more composed than that from D's.

Ban'gyoh laughed proudly—behavior that hardly seemed fitting for a holy man.

Saying nothing, D stared at the flute in his hand, and then gazed at the one the boy had taken and the face of the holy man.

"Hmm. This simply won't do, sir," Ban'gyoh said, backing away with one hand raised. "It's not good to work so hard to cover for one's shortcomings with mere forcefulness. A good-looking man is not the be-all and end-all, you see. Here's a proposition for you—if you want children to favor you over some foolish old priest, you should hang up your sword and live here in their village for the next five years. I bet you'd make the finest mayor they've ever seen!"

Chuckling to himself, Ban'gyoh then walked back to the house. The children had also gone back to the verandah.

Only D and the flute were left out in the stark light.

"For some reason or other, that priest's got it in for you," a hoarse voice could be heard to say from around his left hand as it hung by his side. "But for such an odd duck, he sure says some interesting things. So, how about it? Why don't you settle down here and become head fisherman or something? I'm sure you could get some animal protein out of that huge whale," the voice chortled. After a short pause, he added, "Hey, aren't you gonna tell me to shut up?"

D looked down at his left hand. The oddest expression lingered around his lips. "Head fisherman, eh? That might not be too bad," said the Hunter.

"Wait just a second," shot back a voice tinged with distress. "You wouldn't really . . ." The palm of the left hand was upturned, looking up at D. But soon, the voice let out a sigh. One of relief. "That's a load off my mind. I wouldn't care if you quit here. But wherever you go always ends up being the valley of the shadow of death. You'll keep traveling."

D said nothing.

As if to cut through the roar of the sea, the sound of a child's flute rang out.

II

It was early in the afternoon that the neighbors began to head home. As Su-In stood by the door thanking them, D watched her from the garden. The conversations of a number of the returning guests reached his ears. Dhampirs were said to have hearing three times as good as humans at night and twice as good by day, but apparently this young man's abilities far surpassed even those estimates.

Su-In's gonna be in for a rough time of it.

I wonder what the story is with Wu-Lin?

I hear she went to town, but what awful timing. She'd best hurry back, or Su-In's gonna have a hard time bearing up.

Yeah, they counted on their grandfather an awful lot. He might've had a bum leg, but he sure could do the hypnotism.

You can say that again. When my boy got attacked by a man-eating shark and the shock of it left him bedridden, you wouldn't believe my surprise when he made that child forget all about it in just five minutes.

Su-In's got some pretty mean tricks herself, although there's nothing to use them on out on the open sea.

That's okay. She does all right for herself. And it's downright scary how she throws a harpoon.

You know, I kinda get the feeling Wu-Lin's not coming back.

The other neighbor said nothing.

I wonder if Su-In hasn't really been left on her own after all. My sister was like that when her husband and son went down with their ship. It was exactly the same. Not the tone of her voice or the look in her eye, but the whole atmosphere around her.

"What are you looking so down in the mouth about?" asked a cheery voice that was drawing closer.

As her grandfather's coffin was buried, Su-In hadn't showed any sign of being ready to burst into tears. The last shovelful of earth had covered him an hour ago. She'd had more than enough time to think about how she was going to make ends meet from tomorrow on.

"Your work should be done here until evening. I'm heading out to sea," Su-In said, gazing toward the surf with a faraway look in her eyes. The stern expression she wore was the same one she'd had that morning as she was washing her boat.

"You're going out now?"

"Summer's almost here," the woman replied. "I've got to make some money while I can."

"I'll go, too."

Turning a look of surprise toward his gorgeous face, Su-In said, "But you can't even . . ."

It was common knowledge that those descending from Noble blood would avoid running water. There were villages on the Frontier where the hundreds of houses were all surrounded by individual ditches. While it was understood at present that in order for such ditches to be effective they had to be wide and deep enough to drown an ordinary person, there was still no shortage of people who would waste their energy digging them around their house and wait for rainy days. Out on the sea, the width and depth conditions would be more than met. However, for a dhampir like D—

"I won't have you taking any chances. I don't care how tough my enemies are, they'd never go after me out on the sea."

"One of them rode off into the sky on a cloud," D reminded her.

"Yeah, but . . ."

"I won't get in your way."

Locking her lips together tightly, Su-In glared at D and snorted out her nose. "Okay. But only if you'll stay to one side and not do anything."

The wind at sea sliced at their cheeks. As they weathered gales that made it seem inconceivable that summer would be there in two short days, Su-In's powerboat skipped nimbly across the waves. The sea ahead of them was divided into three distinct sections. Off to the left, a distant fleet of large motorboats gingerly moved in formation. They were catching migratory fish in the black nets that dangled in the water from the stern of the lead vessel. Directly ahead of them and a few miles away, a gigantic form was surrounded by a pack of small powerboats manned by skilled harpooners—and the focus of their massed assault must've been a tidal whale. The surface of the water was tinged with a light pink.

The prow turned to starboard.

"We're cutting in, so it could get a little rough. Be careful you don't fall overboard," Su-In said, her voice full of excitement.

Far ahead of the boat's prow floated a belt of white—a row of ice chunks. As the small boat moved ahead of them, it maneuvered more nimbly than any of the other vessels.

"Giant killer whales are drawn by the whale's blood. Besides the meat on them, their teeth, bones, and innards are all valuable—of course, they might come at the price of your life. Hey, don't tell me you wanna leave already," she joked. Su-In had a lot of pluck—a harsh environment like this wouldn't necessarily suit everyone. There were some women in Florence who would live their whole lives without ever going out to sea, but you could say Su-In was a fierce exception to the rule. This twenty-year-old woman had chosen the most rigorous of battlefields.

The boat rocked, and vermilion stained the water. The battle that'd already been joined was reaching its peak. The water was rough in this part of the sea, where almost a dozen power boats were moving around. The heads and tails of plump game fish came in and out of view as they streaked through the water and slammed against the ships' weak hulls.

"Watch yourself. These bastards can jump over fifteen feet."

Cutting the boat's engine as the vessel rocked from the waves striking it broadside, Su-In released a latch on the deck, scooped up five harpoons, and brought them to the starboard gunwale. Tipped with steel, each of the missiles was seven feet long and weighed over ten pounds. It must've been difficult enough just to hold onto them on the rocking boat. The rough trousers that covered Su-In from the waist down were so taut there wasn't a single wrinkle to them.

Setting four of the harpoons down, Su-In stood ready with the fifth. Hauling back with all her might with her right arm, she used her left hand to support the tip and take aim.

Someone somewhere shouted out her name, the cry echoing on for ages.

A black shape was approaching on the water's surface. A number of harpoons jutted from its top half. When the short, thick head closed to within six or seven feet of Su-In, her upper body leaned back. The shirt she was stuffed into bulged clearly with the shape of her biceps and the muscles on her back. Bracing herself absolutely perfectly, Su-In let the harpoon fly.

The steely missile lanced into the sea with such force you'd swear you heard it sink into flesh, and an instant later the black shape that was approaching twisted wildly. Submerging its impaled head in the sea, it thrashed the water violently with its tail and dorsal fin. Ignoring the massive creature entering its death throes, Su-In got ready with a second harpoon.

"Not too bad, eh?" she called back over her shoulder to D as she shook her head.

The waves kissed her with spray.

"The crease where the head meets the torso is where you make the kill shot. Even most men can't hit it. Here comes another!"

Su-In's scream and the way she collapsed made it clear that her last remark hadn't been directed at the same beast that rammed them a second later. The woman barely managed to pull back her left arm—which dangled out over the gunwale—and used it to prop herself up as a massive black form made a vertical leap just in front of her.

It was certainly huge. And it just kept stretching longer and longer. The glistening wet belly that faced her was the only white thing on it. The tail was forked, and the body must've measured ten feet long and weighed at least sixteen hundred pounds. There was a malicious glint in the tiny eyes to either side of its compact head, and then a long, straight gash opened. Its mouth. It was the color of flames. In midair, the massive creature twisted into an inverted V shape. The turn had been intentional—it was coming back down headfirst.

Su-In was right under it—there wasn't enough time for her to change her position. And yet she managed to look up. Colored by fear and hopelessness, her eyes then reflected a streak of silver that slashed through the mouth ready to close down on her. A powerful tug on her collar hauled her out of the way as the massive form crashed down right in front of her, rocking the hull of the boat.

Realizing as she clung to the Hunter's powerful chest that the giant killer whale's head had been severed from its torso precisely along the line she'd described, Su-In got goose bumps. At the core of her being she ached with a spark that was both feverishly hot and icy cold. On the deck a short distance from her, a sound like steel on steel rose from the head of a beast so thick she'd be lucky to get her arms around it. It was the sound of jagged teeth gnashing. She thought that must be the reason she felt the way she did.

"I suppose I acted out of place," D said, although he didn't really sound all that apologetic.

"No," Su-In said, shaking her head from side to side. She surprised herself that she could even say that much.

"Will one be enough?" he asked. His tone was so calm that she had to wonder where he stored all of his composure.

"Don't be ridiculous. We'll keep taking them till they're all gone." A certain will that even she herself didn't understand had been ignited, and Su-In pulled away from D.

"Hey there!" shouted a familiar voice that cut through the heavy seas.

While it was understandable that Su-In turned in that direction, the fact that D followed her example was highly unusual.

On the prow of the powerboat that ran in parallel to them about forty feet off their port bow, Dwight stood ready with a harpoon in one hand. "Imagine meeting you out here, stud," he called out. "I couldn't have asked for a better setting. I say we finish our duel from yesterday."

Turning to D, Su-In said, "What's he talking about?" She hadn't been informed of the altercation between him and Dwight.

"I owe him," D replied.

Puzzled, Su-In shifted her gaze back and forth between the two men.

"Like I told you before, I'm a fisherman. And out here on the sea, we'll do things my way. You don't have a problem with that, do you?" Dwight said, his right hand around a gleaming harpoon that was longer than Su-In's and almost twice as thick.

From the bridge of the other boat, a young man who probably worked for Dwight was comparing him to D.

D nodded ever so slightly.

"Good enough. We'll each get one throw now. Whoever lands the bigger prize wins. So, give it your best shot," Dwight said, breaking into a grin. "Now, if you lose—well, then you hightail it out of Su-In's house. How does that strike you?"

In lieu of a reply, D took the harpoon from Su-In's hand.

"Hey, wait just a minute! Don't do anything stupid," Su-In angrily shouted at Dwight as she tried to wrest the harpoon from the Hunter. "I don't know what happened between you two, but this guy's working for me and I can't have you doing anything to him."

"This doesn't concern you. It's between him and me—man to man. Stay out of it."

"You big idiot!" the woman shouted indignantly, ready to give him a piece of her mind. But just then there was a terrible impact on the side of the boat. Without even time to leave them with a scream, Su-In toppled over into the water like a log.

"Uh-oh, that's not good!" Dwight shouted, his comment relating to the black shape closing on the woman from behind. Distress rising in his face, his great tree root of a right arm hauled back his harpoon, and then whirled in an arc as he grunted.

Searing through the air, the missile's aim was unerring. Stabbing into the behemoth through its vital point at a thirty-degree angle, the tip came out by the jaw. A geyser of fresh blood shot from the creature's neck as it twisted its body and sank into the sea.

Quickly grabbing a second harpoon, Dwight managed to wring out the words, "How do you like that, hotshot? You might be able to knock me out, but up against one of these monsters you're not good for—"

And then he stopped. He'd just noticed that Su-In's harpoon had vanished from D's right hand. Su-In was clinging to the muscular arm the Hunter had over the side. Behind her, a black mass bobbed to the surface. The harpoon stuck through its neck was clearly Dwight's—a very satisfying hit.

"You blew it, stud," he sneered with one hand to his mouth. "See, Su-In. There's more to a seafaring man than just looks. You need skill on the waves. And I—"

The fisherman's voice died out again. Beside the beast he'd taken, another shape bobbed to the surface. Dwight's eyes went wide—it was a pair of giant killer whales! Seeing that the harpoon that joined them at the neck was one of Su-In's, he couldn't believe his eyes. Even when the strongest of brutes threw a harpoon with all his might, one of these beasts was the most he could ever hope to pierce. The rest would be a matter of accuracy. How skilled did this man have to be to have not only nailed two at once, but to have taken them both through the vital spot?

An attack by a new foe rocked Dwight's boat wildly. As the fisherman's hands hit the deck he looked at D, who'd replaced Su-In at the helm. Staring at the Hunter's handsome profile as he made a run for shore, little by little something dangerously close to a smile spread across Dwight's face.

Just then, the young man at the wheel of his boat screamed, "Wh—what the hell is this?!"

"What is it?" Dwight asked as he turned around.

A trembling hand pointed to the surface of the sea.

"Huh?!" the fearless roughneck exclaimed, but it came as no surprise that his body stiffened with shock when he looked in that direction. There was no problem with the three beasts he and the Hunter had slain, but now black lumps were bobbing to the surface in a bloody swirl with such force it pushed the trio of carcasses away. The other boats might've taken notice of this, as some of them had surrounded the swirl as well.

"What the hell is it?"

"Is that meat?!" someone cried out.

At the very same time, Dwight had also realized that's what it was. "It's meat," he said. "Killer whale meat. Someone's down there ripping one to pieces. Chopping up a damned giant killer whale!"

Oblivious to the cries of the fishermen, chunks of meat continued rising to the surface, but before long that came to an end. Even after the men noticed the bobbing pieces that filled their field of view had edges so clean they looked like they'd been sliced with a knife, not one of them was willing to point that fact out to the others. In the hearts of these men who would live and die on the seas, a certain legend from the past reverberated darkly. They knew perfectly well that legend was tied to their future.

III

Just as the western horizon was stained the color of fresh blood, a woman was climbing out of bed in the town's sole inn. The time she'd spent there and the way she'd spent it remained on her naked skin as a pale, rosy glow that took her seductive beauty to a new level of temptation. It was "Samon of Remembrances."

"Going?" a thick, drowsy voice inquired from right beside her. The body lying back under the sheets contrasted starkly with Samon's own in terms of color and burliness. Like Samon, he was mentally and physically relaxed, but if the need arose his right hand would shoot like lightning for the sword that rested by his pillow.

"You don't have any further need for me, do you?" Samon replied, her answer coming as she put on her underthings. "I've already told you everything I know. And I let you have whatever you wanted in bed, too. Don't embarrass me any further."

"That's funny," he said, his hand shooting up suddenly to grab the woman's hair and yank back on it mercilessly.

Leaving a cry of surprise hanging in the air as she fell on her back, the woman found her face covered by another that was graceful and good-looking. Groans and sighs were exchanged, and then a second later Glen pulled away like he'd been shot from a gun. A thin stream of blood dribbled from his somewhat thick lips, causing vermilion flowers to blossom on the white sheets. Not even bothering to wipe at the part that'd been bitten open, Glen licked the blood from his own lips.

In the meantime, Samon had climbed off the bed.

"You do the damnedest things, don't you? That's the first time a woman's ever wounded me. And my own woman at that," the warrior said, not sounding at all angry.

Samon replied dryly, "I'm not your woman. And I never will be, no matter how many times you may bed me."

"Then what's the story here?"

"I owe you. And until I pay you back, you can have your way."

"Oh, and when do you intend to pay me back?" asked the warrior.

"When I feel like it."

"And how will you pay me back?"

"I'll be the one to decide that, as well," Samon replied. Having finished dressing, she headed for the door.

"Let me just make one thing clear," Glen said as he sat up in bed. Serene as his tone was, it still had enough force to stop Samon in her tracks. "You and your compatriots are free to team up and take him on if you like, but only after I'm through with him. I'll be the one to cut him down. And then you and your friends can take what you want. Otherwise . . ."

"Otherwise what?" Samon said, her eyes glittering. They shone with obvious hostility.

"I'll kill the lot of you before I take him. Even you."

"Even me?" said Samon, her lips curling in a faint smile. "And would you mind if I told my colleagues this?"

"Do what you like. I wouldn't mind fighting the Hunter at my leisure after shooing all the bothersome flies, either."

Samon opened the door. "Do you have anything else to say?" she asked.

"When you and your compatriots decide to take action against him, come to me first."

It was an extremely odd request, but Samon nodded. And then, as if deriding him, she said, "Why don't you just challenge him first?"

"I don't feel like doing that yet."

"Oh, scared, are you?" Samon laughed.

"Is that what you think?" Glen replied, his voice low.

"No. So far as I can see, you're a man without fear. Take care that it doesn't cost you your life."

"Is that supposed to be a warning? You can bring all your friends here if you like," Glen said, his powerful voice rebounding off the back of the now-closed door.

Leaving the inn, Samon headed for the entrance to the village. The stars twinkled above her—the night sky was crystal clear. Only her warrior training kept the breath she exhaled from coming out in a white cloud. When she came to the protective palisade, Samon stopped in her tracks. Casting her tempting gaze above her, she said, "Come on out!"

A colossal tree stood by the side of the road, and one of its massive branches hung right over her head. It didn't have a single leaf on it, but a giant cocoon hung there. Out popped a head. Then the left hand reached smoothly from the casing. No right hand appeared. "Noticed me, did you?" the inverted "Indiscernible Twin" said to her.

"My, but aren't you spry. Egbert's still moaning from his injuries," said Samon. Like her gaze, her voice was an ice-cold needle.

"He got it in the chest, me in the hand—if I had to say which of us was worse off, it'd have to be him. It always pays to learn to disconnect your nerves as early as possible."

"You've been following me, haven't you?"

"Yep," Twin confessed easily. In the starlight, Samon's eyes could clearly make out the slender, boyish face. "I was curious what you were up to. You were going out a lot."

"Orders from Shin, I suppose?"

"My own personal interest, actually," Twin said, cackling like a bird. "This is the first time we've seen each other's faces, but you're quite a fine-looking woman. It's a pity it's night, but then I suppose that suits us more, don't you think?"

"What do you want with me?"

"The guy in that room you were in—he's some sort of drifting warrior, isn't he? What's his connection to you?"

"I don't think I have to tell you that," said Samon.

"At the moment, you're one of our partners in crime. And we can't afford to have even one two-timer in the bunch."

Samon was silent, but her eyes bored right through the inverted figure.

Perhaps noticing as much, Twin cautioned her, "Don't try anything funny. Yesterday we let everyone in on our secret plans. Since we've got so many injured, we decided not to attack for two or three days and rest up instead." His friendly tone died out there. "You wouldn't seriously . . . ," he began to say, but his sharp tone only lasted a second.

Right before his eyes, what looked to be a female form had begun to take shape—upside down, just was he was. As tension and bliss vied for a place on Twin's face, the expression that surfaced there was difficult to describe.

"The thought of me letting you in on my plans when you could never discover them even if you tried," she laughed haughtily. "From the very start I always intended to do this on my own. Anyone who gets in my way gets sent to the next life. The Vampire Hunter, the woman, or the rest of you."

As she said this, Samon slid her right hand into her skirt pocket. The woman before Twin's eyes put her right hand into her long skirt. As proof that the latter was a hallucination, her skirt didn't fly up in accordance with gravity, but stayed just as it would've been if she'd been standing upright. When Samon's right hand shot up again, there was a cold glint from it. A knife gleamed in the phantom woman's hand, too. It couldn't possibly be real. It was an illusion. However, it looked so solid that once it plunged into its target, blood that was all too real would surely gush from the wound. A heartbeat later, the blade that was about to bring death to Twin whipped around suddenly, slashing diagonally through the air. With a hard *clink!* a small stone then fell to the ground at Samon's feet.

"Hold it right there," said a hoarse voice from the other side of the gate.

"Shin—don't tell me you're a skirt-chaser, too?" Samon said, looking over her shoulder.

On the other side of the fence, a human figure as thin as a crane drifted out of the weighty darkness.

Inside, the warrior woman was terribly shaken. She believed she'd been amply careful to prevent being followed, yet two people had tailed her. The only reason she'd noticed Twin was because he'd let his guard down after achieving his aim of finding out where she always went.

"Who was that guy, anyway?"

"Were you looking in on us?" Samon asked. Her tone was hard. The pair hadn't set foot outside the room.

"I see, I hear, I smell, I touch. My eyes are everywhere, and my hands are numberless. I might be the breeze blowing under the door or the moonlight shining in through the window."

"So, what do you intend to do? I suppose you have some problem with this?"

"No. He can go ahead and do what he likes."

Samon knit her brow. She was having difficulty understanding what the interim leader was trying to say.

"It shouldn't come as any great surprise," Shin continued. "Tell him what we're going to do and make it as easy as you can for him. I don't suppose I have to tell you why."

"You mean we'll simply let him do our job?"

"That's right," he said, his voice echoing far and wide in the deep night. "I tangled with him on the ferry on the way over, and he should prove the perfect opponent for a certain Vampire Hunter. All he needs is a fighting chance, and he's sure to kill the Hunter." Laughing, Shin added, "And we're going to take it upon ourselves to make just such a chance for him."

Samon shook her head in disgust. "He won't like that. If he's going to do it, he'll do it alone—that's the sort of man he is."

"Is that what you love about him?" Shin inquired in a lewd tone. "If he's loath to accept any aid, we'll just see to it he doesn't know he's gotten any. Samon, you're to give him our information and keep us posted on his movements."

"Do you seriously think I could do such a thing?"

"Well, I really don't know. That's up to you—or up to him, actually. Glen was the name, wasn't it? You're a prisoner of his manly charms."

Whizzing through the air with blistering speed, a flash of silver linked Samon's hand to the figure.

A cry of pain rang out.

Quickly looking up at the branch above her to confirm that Twin remained under her spell, Samon then dashed toward the fence. Gathering her skirt slightly, she kicked off the ground. Easily clearing the ten-foot-high palisade, as she came back down to earth a black figure lay on the ground just in front of her.

"Not as tough as you make yourself out to be," Samon laughed. But on taking a closer look, she froze. The figure she was so certain had been actual size had become a wooden doll less than eight inches tall with a knife sticking out of it.

"You can't see me. And since you can't, your powers won't work on me," said Shin. His voice rang out from behind her—although it actually sounded more like he was whispering right into her ear. "It's not a bad deal. Whether you love him or hate him, the results are likely to prove equally satisfying. Or would you prefer to die as a traitor? If it comes to that, we'll kill him, too."

Unmoving, Samon seemed to have become part of the night. Shortly thereafter, when Twin had returned from the dreamy world of nostalgia and raced over still sleepy-eyed, a low and unsettling laugh slipped from the warrior woman. "Intriguing," Samon chuckled. "It's none of your business how I feel about him. But I'll tell you what I'd like to see—those two gorgeous men soaked in each other's blood."

†

Elsewhere, around the same time, the voice of the waves echoed around a tiny house overlooking the sea. As if listening to its every word, the gorgeous figure in the yard was motionless, becoming one with the darkness.

The door to the main house opened and lamplight danced on the verandah out back. Holding a long, thin bottle and two glasses in one hand, Su-In called out D's name. She wore an insulated half-coat of dark blue. It was the kind where the inner lining could be filled with hot water to keep it warm. If the lining was made of northern cod intestines, it would hold the heat all day long, but such coats tore quite easily and weren't really suited to rough work.

"Patrolling at this hour?" the woman asked. "Say, you care for a drink? I know it's chilly out, but I can fire up the stove, and the stars are so beautiful."

D climbed up onto the verandah. He might have intended to go to sleep, as his longsword hung from his left hand. He still had his coat on, which was thoroughly in keeping with his character.

Setting the bottle and glasses down on the round top of a little wooden table, Su-In settled back in a chair that was also crafted of wood. With one hand she switched on the oil heater by her feet. She held out a glass filled two-thirds with burgundy-colored liquid, and D accepted it. Not taking a chair, he leaned back against the railing instead.

"I've heard dhampirs don't drink, but I appreciate you humoring me. All you have to do is hold it. Just to set the mood," Su-In said.

Swallowing a mouthful, she turned her attention to D's longsword. The glass was in his left hand. His longsword was leaning against the railing.

"Always keep your right hand free—isn't that the warrior way? That's the way all the ones who came through the village were. That's a strange sword, though."

D didn't reply.

Not seeming to mind, Su-In continued, "I've never seen a sword curved like that before. Where was it made? You sure travel around, don't you? All alone . . ."

Her glass rose again, and her throat bobbed.

Suddenly letting his eyes drop from her drink, D said, "There's work again tomorrow."

Eyes going wide, Su-In set her glass down and exhaled violently. "Don't startle me like that," she exclaimed. "Why, the very thought of you caring about anyone else. Okay, even if you do worry about me, don't ever say it out loud. It'll ruin your image. Or could it be you're worried my getting drunk will make your job tougher?"

"That's right."

Su-In shut her eyes. Pulling the front of her fur-trimmed coat shut, she said, "The harsh truth. It really hits hard tonight, that's for sure. But I understand how it is. I can't get too dependent on you. After all, someday you'll be gone."

Her eyes turned upward, catching D. He was staring out toward the garden. Maybe he was watching the stars.

"It's okay, you don't have to worry," the woman told him. "Grampa's not gonna come back as some sort of monster. There're two more graves beside his, right? My mother's and father's. I'm sure they're all swapping jokes in the hereafter."

There was no reply from the Hunter.

Su-In continued gulping down the contents of her glass. "My mother and father died at sea," she said. "Got rammed by a monster of a giant killer whale before they could finish it off. Their bodies never came back up. So those graves are just markers. I bet Grampa can't even talk to them. But it's still better than Wu-Lin. Poor girl . . . I can't even make a grave for her," Su-In said, something gleaming in her eye.

That was something she personally had decided after talking to D. Everything would come out after those who sought the bead had been dealt with and the secrets of the bead had been solved—it would avoid causing any more complications. But Wu-Lin's funeral would have to wait until then.

Su-In gazed at D, a fierce light in her eyes. "You're gonna outlive me, right?" she said to him. "Chances are I could wind up just like Wu-Lin. If it comes to that, I'd like you to make me a grave. You'll probably be the last person to ever see me or my sister . . ."

The surface of the wine in D's glass didn't display even the tiniest ripple.

"You're going to hide," D said succinctly.

"Where?"

"I'm sure Dwight would be glad to give you some advice on that," D replied.

"Don't get the wrong idea about the two of us."

"They should know by now that I have the bead. The only use they'd have for you from here on out is as a hostage."

"You don't pull any punches, do you? But I don't wanna do that," Su-In said. "I'll be damned if I'm gonna run and hide. Especially not from the bastards that killed my sister. I know there's no way I could beat them in a fight, but I at least want them to know they don't scare me. What's more—"

D turned and gazed at Su-In.

"Thanks to you bagging three big ones for me, I can get by this summer without going out fishing. So I've got a school to run."

Keeping silent for a bit, D finally said, "That's fine."

"Thanks for going along with my decision. It's always reassuring to have someone on your side."

"When does school start?" asked the Hunter.

"The day after tomorrow. Tomorrow's the schoolhouse's grand opening ceremony."

"What do you teach?"

"Are you interested?" Su-In blinked her eyes. Her cheeks were a little flushed. "If we had a teacher like you, we'd be in serious trouble. Oh, the problems we'd have with students falling in love with you. I bet the grades would be the worst ever. Since you ask, I do math and social studies at the moment."

"By social studies, do you mean history?"

"No, geography. The kids are really looking forward to it. If you like, why don't you teach them something?"

D didn't say anything.

Sighing, Su-In set down her glass and stared at her own hand. "I can hold chalk," she said, "but a brush is pretty tricky with hands like these."

Big and thick as any man's, her hands were covered with calluses all the way to the fingertips. Hauling nets, throwing harpoons, washing boats—she'd been doing these things since childhood. After a whole decade of such work, even a woman would earn toughened hands. Su-In took her index finger and tapped it against the table. Over and over, there was the sound of wood striking wood.

"You know, I wanted to be an artist," she said plainly.

"There aren't any pictures in your house, though."

"I burnt them all up, right after my parents' funeral was over. I think the only reason I'm here today is because I did that." She went on to explain that Wu-Lin had only been nine at the time, and her grandfather had already reached the point where everyday life was tough enough for him.

"I heard your grandfather helped people with hypnotism."

"Not that he could do much with it," Su-In countered quickly. "When folks work out on the wintry sea, there's not much you can accomplish just by looking in their eyes. All Grampa Han could do was ease their remaining pain some."

"That's enough," D replied. "It's better than just staying sad."

"I think so," Su-In said, power in her voice. "A few people forgot all about crying, thanks to Grampa. But after about six months, they'd come back in tears and beg him to make them remember again. I don't know the exact reason why. But I get the feeling I understand. People can forget all kinds of sad things. But some things are just so sad, they have to be remembered . . ." Su-In's words died out there. "Why are you looking at me like that?" she asked.

"Did your grandfather use his hypnotism all of the time?"

Su-In shook her head. "After *that* happened a few times, he just gave it up completely." An ambiguous expression flitted across her round face. A memory had come back to her. Most likely, Su-In herself didn't know whether that was good or bad. "Oh, that's right . . . ," she said dreamily. "There was this one time . . . about six months ago, I said to Grampa it'd been five years since he'd used his hypnotism . . . and he said that no, there'd been this one time about three years ago when he'd used it just once . . ."

"Who did he use it on?" D inquired.

"Just a second—I remember it clearly . . . I asked him that very same thing. That's right. But he never answered me. I always did wonder about that, though."

"Do you have any idea who it might've been?"

"No."

"You should get some sleep," D said as he pulled away from the handrail.

"You're really not gonna drink that, are you?" Su-In said somewhat bitterly, raising the other glass to her mouth. But it stopped short. With incredible willpower she returned the glass to the table. "I suppose you're right," she said to the Hunter. "I'll pass on that. A fisherman's one thing, but for a teacher to reek of booze wouldn't be good."

"You're right," D said, slowly stepping down from the verandah.

"D," Su-In called out to him in a low voice.

Not turning, D asked her what she wanted.

"Nothing. That's a good name you have."

"Good night."

Not saying another word, Su-In followed his back with her eyes as he walked away to the barn. Even after the figure of beauty had disappeared through the entrance and the door had shut, the woman didn't move for the longest time.

To be continued in

VAMPIRE HUNTER D
VOLUME 8
MYSTERIOUS JOURNEY TO THE NORTH SEA
PART TWO

available September 2007

About the Author

Hideyuki Kikuchi was born in Chiba, Japan in 1949. He attended the prestigious Aoyama University and wrote his first novel *Demon City Shinjuku* in 1982. Over the past two decades, Kikuchi has authored numerous horror novels, and is one of Japan's leading horror masters, writing novels in the tradition of occidental horror authors like Fritz Leiber, Robert Bloch, H. P. Lovecraft, and Stephen King. As of 2004, there are seventeen novels in his hugely popular ongoing Vampire Hunter D series. Many live action and anime movies of the 1980s and 1990s have been based on Kikuchi's novels.

About the Illustrator

Yoshitaka Amano was born in Shizuoka, Japan. He is well known as a manga and anime artist and is the famed designer for the Final Fantasy game series. Amano took part in designing characters for many of Tatsunoko Productions' greatest cartoons, including *Gatchaman* (released in the U.S. as *G-Force* and *Battle of the Planets*). Amano became a freelancer at the age of thirty and has collaborated with numerous writers, creating nearly twenty illustrated books that have sold millions of copies. Since the late 1990s Amano has worked with several American comics publishers, including DC Comics on the illustrated Sandman novel *Sandman: The Dream Hunters* with Neil Gaiman and *Elektra and Wolverine: The Redeemer* with best-selling author Greg Rucka for Marvel Comics.

The first book in a highly successful series of novels from Japan,
Blood: The Last Vampire—Night of the Beasts
is a startling, fast-paced thriller full of chilling surprises.

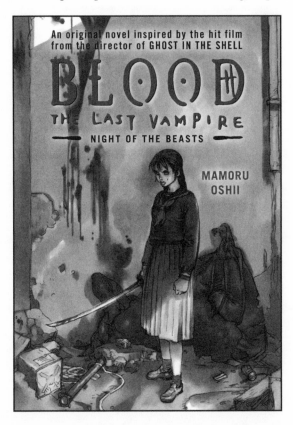

An original novel inspired by the hit film
from the director of GHOST IN THE SHELL

BLOOD

THE LAST VAMPIRE

NIGHT OF THE BEASTS

MAMORU
OSHII

At Yokota Base in Japan, American soldiers stand guard at the brink of the Vietnam War. Although they fear the enemy outside their base, an even more dangerous enemy waits within—bloodthirsty vampires walk among them! Saya, a fierce and beautiful vampire hunter, leads a team of undercover agents who must wipe out the vampires before they can wipe out the base. But even though Saya is a powerful warrior, her ferocity may not be enough!

ISBN-10: 1-59582-029-9 / ISBN-13: 978-1-59582-029-7 | $8.95

AVAILABLE AT YOUR LOCAL COMICS SHOP OR BOOKSTORE
To find a comics shop in your area, call 1-888-266-4266
For more information or to order direct: •On the web: darkhorse.com •E-mail: mailorder@darkhorse.com
•Phone: 1-800-862-0052 Mon.-Fri. 9 A.M. to 5 P.M. Pacific Time.
BLOOD THE LAST VAMPIRE: NIGHT OF THE BEASTS (KEMONO TACHI NO YORU BLOOD THE LAST VAMPIRE) © Mamoru Oshii 2000. © Production I.G. 2000.
Originally published in Japan in 2000 by KADOKAWA SHOTEN PUBLISHING Co., Ltd., Tokyo. English Translation rights arranged with KADOKAWA SHOTEN
PUBLISHING Co., Ltd., Tokyo through TOHAN CORPORATION, Tokyo. DH Press™ is a trademark of Dark Horse Comics, Inc. All rights reserved. (BL7000)
dhpressbooks.com